Inventing Victoria

ALSO BY TONYA BOLDEN

Finding Family

Crossing Ebenezer Creek

Facing Frederick: The Life of Frederick Douglass,
A Monumental American Man

Pathfinders: The Journeys of Sixteen Extraordinary Black Souls

Capital Days: Michael Shiner's Journal and the Growth of
Our Nation's Capital

Beautiful Moon: A Child's Prayer

Searching for Sarah Rector: The Richest Black Girl in America

Emancipation Proclamation: Lincoln and the Dawn of Liberty

George Washington Carver

M.L.K.: Journey of a King

Maritcha: A Nineteenth Century American Girl

Cause: Reconstruction America, 1863–1877

The Champ: The Story of Muhammad Ali

Portraits of African-American Heroes

We Are Not Yet Equal (with Carol Anderson)

Inventing Victoria

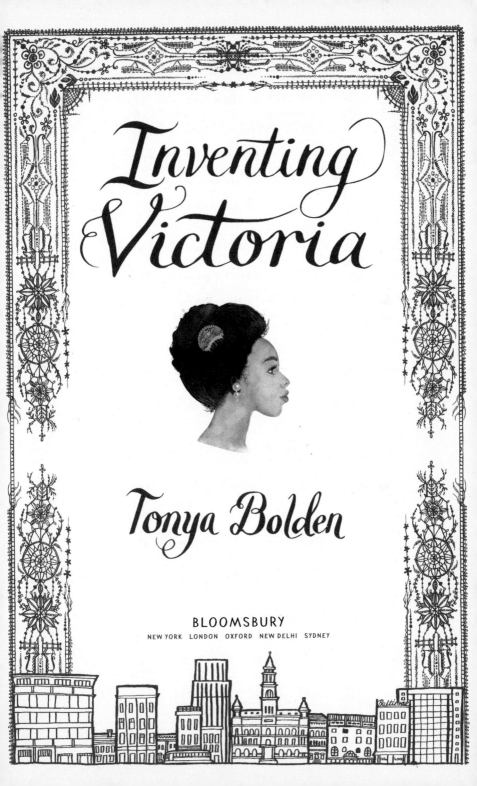

Tonya Bolden

BLOOMSBURY

NEW YORK   LONDON   OXFORD   NEW DELHI   SYDNEY

BLOOMSBURY YA
Bloomsbury Publishing Inc., part of Bloomsbury Publishing Plc
1385 Broadway, New York, NY 10018

BLOOMSBURY and the Diana logo are trademarks of Bloomsbury Publishing Plc

First published in the United States of America in January 2019 by Bloomsbury YA

Bloomsbury books may be purchased for business or promotional use. For information
on bulk purchases please contact Macmillan Corporate and Premium Sales Department at
specialmarkets@macmillan.com

Library of Congress Cataloging-in-Publication Data
Names: Bolden, Tonya, author.
Title: Inventing Victoria / by Tonya Bolden.
Description: New York : Bloomsbury, 2019.
Summary: Essie, a young black woman in 1880s Savannah, is offered
the opportunity to leave her shameful past and be transformed
into an educated, high-society woman in Washington, D.C.
Identifiers: LCCN 2018024642 (print) | LCCN 2018031860 (e-book)
ISBN 978-1-68119-807-1 (hardcover) • ISBN 978-1-68119-808-8 (e-book)
Subjects: | CYAC: Identity—Fiction. | African Americans—Fiction. | Reconstruction
(U.S. history, 1865–1877)—Fiction. | Savannah (Ga.)—History—19th century—Fiction. |
Washington (D.C.)—History—19th century—Fiction.
Classification: LCC PZ7.B635855 Inv 2019 (print) | LCC PZ7.B635855 (e-book) |
DDC [Fic]—dc23
LC record available at https://lccn.loc.gov/2018024642

Book design by John Candell
Typeset by Westchester Publishing Services
Printed and bound in the U.S.A. by Berryville Graphics Inc., Berryville, Virginia
2 4 6 8 10 9 7 5 3 1

To find out more about our authors and books visit www.bloomsbury.com
and sign up for our newsletters.

Inventing Victoria

BROODING, WINDSWEPT SKY

"For as much as it has pleased Almighty God to take out of this world the soul of . . ."

As Essie stood beneath a brooding, windswept sky there was a twinge of guilt over being dry-eyed.

Another emotion quickly took hold as the bewhiskered, bucktoothed Reverend Zephaniah McElroy droned on.

Panic.

The past was snatching Essie back.

SAVANNAH RIVER TOO

Back to a tattered room on Factors Row, a room smelling of cigars, whiskey, sweat.

Savannah River too.

Back to a closet with a pallet for her sleep.

Some nights?

Most nights?

Back to sleep never coming quickly enough after Mamma poured a hot, bitter drink down her throat, plugged cotton in her ears.

Back to . . .

SLIPWAYS TO THE PAST

Reverend McElroy's voice was high, cracked. "We therefore commit her body . . ."

Wrenched free from the past, Essie gazed up at live oaks weeping Spanish moss.

A fairly decent send-off. That's something.

To where?

Had there been even a whiff of repentance with that last or next-to-last breath?

Clearly Reverend McElroy's church hadn't thought so. It tolerated a graveside funeral but not a burial among its parishioners. So it was that they were on the outskirts of the cemetery, in Strangers' Ground.

Reverend McElroy.

Gravedigger Bogins.

Gravedigger Scriven.

Binah.

Ma Clara.

Essie shifted from foot to foot, willed herself to sail into her dream coming true, her rescue from a life of pitiful prospects. Her magnificent black mourning dress bore witness to that. Yet, even while surrendering to a moment of delight over that fancy black dress—in her wishes having wings—Essie still couldn't keep her mind from finding slipways to the past.

UNCLE PERCIVAL, UNCLE . . .

Back to the whisper: "It'll make for sweet dreams."

Like quiet, sweet dreams were rare. Nightmares mostly.

Of running.

Struggling to breathe.

Trapped in a sack, desperately trying to bite, claw her way out.

Back to slivers of time between sleep and wake violated by terrifying noises from the street.

Cussing.

Glass shattering.

Fists pounding flesh.

Gurgling.

Feet running fast.

More sickening were the sounds from the other side of the closet door in that tattered room on Factors Row.

Hungry grunts.

Huffing, puffing, panting.

Mamma crying out, "Oh, mercy!"

Bedsprings squeaked something awful. Now fast. Now slow.

Uncle Percival.

Uncle Eldred.

Uncle Judd.

ESPECIALLY UNCLE FRITZ

Back to stairs creaking when uncles tromped up, tromped down.

Especially Uncle Fritz with the clubfoot and that cane of his sporting a frightening Bird Man handle that could take out an eye.

How can white menfolks be uncles? Essie wondered once she was old enough to start sifting out distinctions. *Maybe*, she reasoned, *maybe they light-skinned colored like me. Only lighter.*

Brothers of the pa she never knew?

Brothers of Mamma?

Neither idea sat right.

Was she five, six?

Bewildered, scared, Essie often cried herself to sleep.

SALTBOX HOUSE ON MINIS STREET

Back to mornings of chains clanking; brute, bossy voices; horses clip-clopping, clip-clopping.

And the uncles kept coming.

More after Mamma moved them into that saltbox house on Minis Street, a house shared with aunties Katy and Emma.

One skinny, coffee-bean brown with Cherokee cheeks, a sly smile. The other close to pecan in color. More meat on her bones. Weasel eyes.

Like Mamma, the aunties slept heaps and heavy when the sun was out. Afternoons they most times lollygagged in the parlor wearing sheer gowns or brightly colored robes over camisoles and pantaloons.

Sipping whiskey.

Playing cards.

Bragging.

Telling lies.

Soon to get gussied up for the uncles.

At least Essie no longer slept in a closet some nights, most nights. In that house on Minis Street she had the tiny attic all to herself.

A meager, miserable room early on. Moss-stuffed mattress atop a narrow wrought-iron bed. Small battered dull blue sea chest at its foot. Painted on its inside lid a three-masted schooner.

That seafaring scene called to little Essie. Many a night she wished that she was on that ship or at least that the sea chest was large enough for her to climb into, shut the lid, shut out all the noises rising from below.

Cackling.

Cussing.

Gutter laughter.

Mamma or an auntie, perched on the red velvet, gold-tasseled stool, banging away on that decrepit melodeon.

Essie was back to wanting to scream.

FAR, FAR AWAY FROM
FOREST CITY

She blinked as wicked winds whipped through Strangers' Ground. Spanish moss seemed in a right frenzy to be free.

And Essie saw herself all those years ago, curled up in the attic's dormer window seat, gazing out at the night.

Some nights sweltering.

Other nights cold.

During hailstorms, rainstorms, lightning like cannon blasts.

So lonely.

Essie saw herself longing to be far, far away from that house on Minis Street—far, far away from Forest City.

Most of all she had ached to be somebody else's child.

FIRST RESCUE, FIRST REFUGE

"Earth to earth . . ."

On Wednesday, July 13, 1881, standing there in Strangers' Ground, when Essie caught herself wringing her hands, gritting her teeth, she switched her mind to what she had to get done within the next few days.

Sort out the house on Minis Street.

Finish up with Lawyer Logan.

Teach the new girl the boardinghouse rules.

Buy a leather traveling bag from Clapp's.

Pack.

Give Ma Clara a surprise, Binah some clothes.

In just a few days Essie would be gone from Forest City.

Beneath her dense black veil she allowed herself a smile.

But then she looked over at Binah, first and only friend.

A lump arose in Essie's throat after a glance at bandy-legged Ma Clara. Ma Clara with twinkling eyes, gray hair like a crown, skin darker than a moonless winter midnight. Ever since she could remember, the old woman came twice a week to clean that house on Minis Street. Ma Clara had been her first rescue, first refuge. She had so much to thank her for, starting with . . .

TOO MUCH RED

"School?"

Mamma was primping and preening at her dressing table.

Ma Clara stood in the doorway with a dusty blue full apron over a brown plaid dress. A cinnamon head wrap covered her hair.

"Yes, Praline, *school*. So Essie can get proper book learning, learn her sums and such. She's a bright one." Ma Clara had taught Essie the alphabet, had her reading small words.

Peeking from behind Ma Clara's skirt, doe-eyed, sandy-haired Essie, all of seven, sent up a hallelujah for the timing. When Mamma was getting ready for the night, especially a Friday night, she was bound to say yes to *anything*.

Essie crossed her fingers behind her back as she watched Mamma—hair done up, rouge on cheeks and lips—stand, tighten her corset, strap on a bustle.

"School cost money?" Mamma commenced wiggling and squirming into a screaming hot-pink ball gown with black lace trim.

"Beach Institute is a dollar a month," replied Ma Clara. "Best one around here for colored."

Mamma sniffed.

"And if you ask me Essie deserves the best," Ma Clara added.

Essie hoped to be as strong as Ma Clara one day. Though Mamma had her hard face on, Essie had a hunch that deep down she was afraid of Ma Clara.

Mamma stepped into scarlet spool-heeled silk shoes with pink rosettes on the toes.

Little Essie hardly ever went into Mamma's room. It made her stomach hurt, brought a tightness to her chest. Too much red.

Curtains red.

Bedspread red.

Wallpaper worse. Blood-red with a crowd of giant pink and gold peonies in a wild, wicked dance.

"I guess it be okay," Mamma finally said, dabbing scent behind her ears.

Essie raced up to her room, looked in her mirror. In this magical moment the flecks of green in her hazel eyes sparkled.

"I'm going to school!" She jumped up and down. "I'm going to school!"

L-A-U-D—

Essie was a new penny those first few days, a jumble of jubilee over the fact that, though bleary-eyed and grumpy, Mamma got her ready for school. Mamma had even bought her two new dresses, a tartan green and a calico blue, along with a pair of bone-colored high-top side-button shoes.

Essie thought she glimpsed a rise of pride in Mamma's eyes as she headed off to school.

Didn't last.

"Lemme lone," Mamma grunted when Essie tried to wake her on a Monday within weeks of her starting school, where Miss Purdy, in a crisp white blouse and black or gray skirt, made everybody sit up straight and began each lesson with "Well, now, boys and girls . . ."

On that "Lemme lone" Monday Essie spotted an empty pink bottle on Mamma's bedroom floor. She picked it up.

L-A-U-D—

Mysterious word. Essie couldn't make it out. The longer she stared at the skull and crossbones on the label the more her stomach hurt. Trembling, she laid the bottle on the dressing table, dashed from the room.

Face washed, teeth cleaned with a finger and some bicarb soda, Essie pulled out a dress from the wicker basket in a corner of her bedroom. She opened the window, waved the dress in the air, put it on. Lickety-split she was downstairs in the kitchen dabbing vanilla extract behind her ears and, here and there, on her green dress. That's when she saw the Catawba jam stain on the back. Right where she sat.

Essie wiped at the stain with a wet dishrag, but the red wouldn't go away.

It only went pink.

What started out looking like a pond became an ocean.

Back up in her room Essie took off her dress, turned it inside out, put it back on. Then she grabbed her satchel, bounded down the stairs. On the last step, a heel broke off.

Her stomach was a boat on a tempest-tossed sea as she fought back tears. She could keep on going or head back up to her room and change into her mud-colored canvas shoes.

Miss Purdy whacked your hand with a ruler if you were late.

Essie decided to keep on going. She hobbled fast to school.

FREEWILLUM!

"Essie is messy! Essie is messy!" chanted Sarah Pace during recess that day. "And look at those crookedy-crookedy plaits!"

Essie's stomach growled.

Sarah Pace howled with laughter, waved other kids over. Then she wagged a finger in Essie's face, the finger of her right hand on the back of which was a birthmark shaped like a heart. "Essie is messy!" taunted this chestnut girl with wide-set, witching eyes, hooded lids. "Gutter girl!" she yelled.

Surrounded, Essie burst into tears.

"Essie is messy! Essie is messy! Essie is messy!" the children chanted.

Ma Clara came to the rescue again. She persuaded Mamma to let Essie stay by her on weekends.

*   *   *

Had Essie known the word "halcyon," that's how she would have described her days on Shad Island. There, in Ma Clara's tabby cottage, she learned to tend to herself better, from washing her clothes to washing and plaiting her hair, there on that tiny island where it seemed everybody except Ma Clara was Geechee, like her second husband had been and like ferryman Jack was, ferryman Jack who always sang the same song, going to, going fro.

"Freewillum!" the tall, reedy man shouted out. "Gwine home to sine de oshun. . . . Freewillum!"

"Freewillum!" Essie sometimes sang to herself during Shad Island days as she drew pictures in the sand, trawled for crawfish, helped Ma Clara make Frogmore Stew. That's how Essie said thank you.

And, come nightfall, by readying things for Ma Clara's foot soak. When that was over, Essie rubbed the old woman's ankles and knees with liniment, then her hands and feet with a rosemary and rosewater balm.

"A life of hard toil sure takes a toll," Ma Clara sometimes said as she slipped her feet into the wooden tub of hot water sprinkled with lovage and lavender. "Essie, do make something of yourself," she urged. "True, life is hard on us colored, but any chance come your way to rise in life you must be like a dog with a bone so you don't end up all broke down when old."

Essie sat beside Ma Clara on a driftwood stool or cross-legged on the floor, always hungry for the love and eager for wisdom and stories, even though some of them left Essie with a hurting heart. Like the one about the Weeping Time.

"They say if not the largest it was one of the largest sales of slaves by a single planter. Ole Pierce Butler, who didn't even live down here but up in Philadelphia."

They were before the hearth, Essie almost done greasing Ma Clara's scalp.

"High living, gambling, and speculations—buying things he thought would rise in value—Ole Pierce Butler was drowning in debt, had to sell slaves. Over four hundred souls, some from his cotton planation on St. Simon's. Some from his rice plantation near Darien. All born there, many like their people before them."

Essie was ready to start cornrowing the old woman's hair.

"It was an April day—no, in March—when they crammed those poor souls into stalls out at the race track. Most field hands, others carpenters, blacksmiths, house servants. Some old like I am now. Some babies. I believe only one family was fortunate to be bought by one person."

Essie's fingers moved quickly, her parts were straight.

"That auction lasted for two days. And the whole time it rained, steady, heavy. Only after the last group of slaves stepped down from the auction block did the wind and rain cease. That's why we call it the Weeping Time. God was crying right along with us."

Essie was herself close to crying as she imagined all the tears colored shed during slavery days.

Tears filling oceans.

Stories like that of the Weeping Time always made Essie so glad that she wasn't white, no matter Ma Clara had told her that not all whitefolks were vipers. "Some was our friends," she had said one day. "Senator Charles Sumner, William Lloyd Garrison, Lydia Maria Child. Lots of Quakers."

Still, as Essie thanked God that she hadn't known slavery, she continued to thank him that she wasn't white. She didn't like her color, didn't like being so close in color to the uncles. She wished she was all-African like Ma Clara, like ferryman Jack, like everybody else on Shad Island seemed to be.

It was on Shad Island that Ma Clara also told Essie why her friend Old Man Boney, drayman and lamplighter, didn't have a real home to speak of.

"His carts is his home." Ma Clara then explained that Old Man Boney had been one of the thousands of colored folks who got acres from the government during the war. "Land in Carolina, Florida, Georgia too. Lowcountry land all for colored people only."

Old Man Boney's land had been on Skidaway Island.

"Had built himself a nice little home, outbuildings. He'd sown crops. Was ready to ask his sweetheart to marry him when government men came to say the land was no longer his and was going back to secesh men. He didn't want any kind of regular home after that, didn't trust that some white man wouldn't take it away."

Reverend Zephaniah McElroy hiccuped.

That snatched Essie back to . . .

THE BACKHAND SLAP

"You ungrateful little heifer!"

Essie had pretended to not see the bloodstains on Mamma's pantaloons when her dressing gown flew open with the backhand slap.

Minutes earlier Essie stood in the archway to the kitchen, eyes on the floor.

"I got work, Mamma. Be moving out."

Mamma, squinty-eyed, was slouched in a chair at the kitchen table, a bag of taffy and a cup of black coffee before her. She hiccuped, then asked, "Work?" She hiccuped again. "What kind of work?"

"Ma Clara got me a place at Abby Bowfield's."

"Who that?"

"Over on Bryan, a boardinghouse. Ma Clara said Miss Abby's rheumatism plagues her something awful, so she can't do like she used to." Essie knew the details would be lost on

Mamma, but she reckoned that if she kept talking she'd keep up her nerve. "More than that, Miss Abby's number-one maid is about to get married, moving to Brunswick. Pays good, five dollars a week, plus room and—"

On the tail end of another hiccup Mamma looked Essie up and down scornful-like. "You leavin' from here to be a damn servant?" She rose.

Essie took a step back. "Miss Abby's is an upstanding place."

"Mean to tell me I done raised a fool?"

You didn't raise me at all, Essie thought. *Ma Clara did that.*

"You rather scrub floors and empty piss pots than—"

Essie blazed with rage. "At least it's honest work!"

Slap!

Essie had figured on a peaceful parting, thought Mamma would be glad to have the attic free of her. She could do it up in red, rent it out to a girl eager to shift from walking the waterfront.

Face stinging, Essie spun around, made for her room.

Mamma followed.

"You, what, all of thirteen now and you think you a woman?" By then Mamma was at the top of the stairs.

"Fourteen," Essie said softly. "Old enough to make my own way." She removed clothing from the highboy, placed it on her bed. From beneath it, she retrieved an old carpetbag found in the shed.

Mamma sucked her teeth. "You and your 'at least it's honest work' . . . I'm more honest than a helluva lot of women." She was inside the room by now. "Heaps of women get with men for money, only they call theyselves wives."

Essie stepped over to her wardrobe, brought out her few dresses, her other pair of shoes. She was determined to not let Mamma get a rise out of her again.

"You stuck-up little . . . That Clara Wiggins . . . Teachin' you to look down on me."

Essie kept packing her bag. "Ma Clara *never* run you down. If anything—"

Mamma flounced over to the bed. "If anythin' what?"

"Nothing."

"If anythin' *what?*" Mamma was breathing hard.

"If anything . . . ," Essie began sheepishly. "If anything Ma Clara feels sorry for you."

"Feels sorry for me?" Mamma tightened the belt of her dressing gown, put her hands on her hips, poked out her mouth. "That ole witch . . . she got some nerve . . . Ma Clara this, Ma Clara that. *I'm* your ma!"

Essie bit her tongue.

Mamma sauntered over to the window. "You know, you remind me of a gal I met on Sherman's March."

Essie glanced at the back of Mamma, at the orange zinnias on her scarlet dressing gown, then down at her dirty feet.

"A real Goody Two-shoes," Mamma continued. "But

guess what? She didn't make it to Savannah while I *did*."
Mamma thumped her chest, whipped around. "And you
know why?"

Essie looked away.

"I had value to Yankee soldiers. Hid me in a wagon.
That's how I got across Ebenezer Creek, how I came to not
wind up dead or drug back to slavery." She picked at a scab
on the back of her hand. "I was good to Yankee soldiers.
Yankee soldiers was good to me." Mamma looked like she
had won a blue ribbon at a county fair.

I was good to Yankee soldiers.

Years ago Essie had asked if one of the uncles was her
pa. Mamma had given her a flat no. After that, Essie had
been too scared to ask who was.

Now Essie did the math, factoring in her color and
Mamma's coppery skin. Sherman's army reached Savannah
in late '64 she knew. She had been born on August 15, '65,
or sometime that week Mamma had told her. "My father
was a Yankee soldier? A white man?" Essie finally asked,
bag almost packed.

"Sure was." Mamma looked proud.

"Who was he—what was his name?" Essie blurted out
before concluding, *What difference does it make?*

Mamma shrugged. "I always hoped it was the one with
the last name Mirth. Tall, blond hair. Wasn't much to look
at but was real gen'rous. Liked him the most. That's why I
took his last name."

Essie shook her head.

"Yes, siree," Mamma said softly. "Keepin' Yankee soldiers happy was keepin' alive and havin' less hardship."

Essie could feel Mamma's eyes on her. The back of her neck tingled.

"Anyway, I could have losed you."

"Losed me?"

"There's ways to keep a baby from comin'. But I didn't do none of that. I let you live, gave you life. This how you repay me?"

"Mamma, I just want to—"

"You ever been without a roof over your head?"

"No."

"Ever gone hungry?"

Again Essie said no, though at times she had. The larder and the shelves were full or bare depending on Mamma's state of mind. On a good day breakfast might be eggs, grits, ham, biscuits and supper Limpin' Susan or fried shad, red rice, and cabbage. Other days for breakfast Essie made do with a few pickles or a stale biscuit with a dab of butter or Catawba jam. Some nights supper was a can of Borden's condensed milk or an onion and some salt pork Essie fried up. Thank goodness for those days on Shad Island. Essie never wondered if she'd get a bellyful there.

"So why you up and leavin'?" Mamma folded her arms across her chest.

Essie was perplexed. *Mamma cares?* No, she decided. Just vexed over Ma Clara's connection to her leaving. The only other time Mamma had slapped Essie was years back when she begged to live at Ma Clara's every day of the week.

Essie made a mental note to get a croker sack for her wall shelf and the books and magazines it held.

Mamma grabbed her by the face. "Answer me, you little heifer. Why you up and leavin'?"

Essie pulled away, wiped her face with the back of her hand, then let loose the riot in her mind. "You really want to know why I'm leaving, Mamma? Because I'm sick of this house! Sick of finding you laid out like dead in the parlor or on your bedroom floor from whiskey or laudanum!"

Mamma seemed stunned.

"Sick of how your white men look at me!" Essie continued. "How some try to pat me, telling me what a pretty little thing I am. Just sick of it all!" Essie looked away, lowered her voice. "I want my own life, Mamma—a *better* life, a *new* life!"

There was yelling, too, from a house next door. Mr. and Mrs. Rakestraw at each other's throats again. Something to do with money and a hussy on Congress Street.

"Well, you is a right pretty gal," Mamma finally said. "Fine grade of hair. Nice shape. Long legs. And with your color men pay twice what they pay for Katy and Emma. More than they pay for me."

Thank God for Ma Clara, Essie thought. *Thank God I'm getting out of this house!*

"You could do worse!" Mamma pressed on, back in Essie's face. "How many colored women you know own a home like this free and clear? Some weekends I make more money than your precious Clara Wiggins make in a fortnight."

Again she paced.

"It's hard for a colored woman who got no family, no husband. 'Specially with all the promises about true freedom snatched away. Like how back long years ago our men got the vote, but most is kept from it by night riders and schemes. My white men, they my protection. Your protection, too, so long as you under my roof. As I was risin' I was plannin' for us."

Essie had, of course, noticed that Mamma's white men had long ago ceased to be sailors, dockworkers, watchmen. They were lawmen, bankers, politicians, doctors, businessmen, and the like. It never dawned on Essie that it had been planned. She had never thought Mamma capable of planning *anything*.

But then what did she know about Mamma other than that she came to Savannah on General William Tecumseh Sherman's famous march to the sea, that she loved taffy and liverwurst, and, of all things, doing laundry when in a steady state of mind. "Calms my nerves," she once said.

Mamma never talked about her days in slavery, who her people were, nothing like that. It also dawned on Essie that this was the longest conversation that she and Mamma had ever had.

* * *

Mamma looked around the attic. "That bed of yours. Highboy. Nightstand. Washstand. Wardrobe. Gifts from Mr. Farquhar who got that furniture store on Broughton."

The attic had been Essie's sanctuary, the only place in that house on Minis Street where she had felt safe. She had taken pride in keeping it clean, sweeping and mopping, polishing the furniture. The five-drawer highboy, with its mirror's frame fashioned like a harp, was her delight.

Gifts from Mr. Farquhar who got that furniture store on Broughton.

So her bedroom was tainted, soiled, dirty, too, like everything else in this accursed house.

"Country ham you love . . . china dishes you eat off . . . wallpaper in the parlor . . . piano . . . clothes you packin'."

Everything was filthy. Everything except Essie's wall shelf, her books and magazines, things she'd gotten on her own.

Essie thought about grabbing them and leaving everything else behind, then quickly figured that foolish. But she vowed that after she started earning money at Miss Abby's she'd get herself some new clothes—outfits to underthings—and burn every bit of clothing Mamma had bought for her. Hair ribbons too.

Mamma was in her face again. "You got a problem with how I earn a livin', but you never had a problem with the gifts I gets from my genelmen friends." She flicked the coral necklace around Essie's neck. "Or the things my money buy."

"Mamma, I just want to go my own way."

Essie watched Mamma pace again. "Ever since you start smellin' yo'self, you been lookin' down on me. Too good to pat Juba or do a little jig and whatnot, learn to play the harmonicky or a ditty on the piano. No, you always somewhere with your nose in a book. Too good to even give my genelmen friends a smile." She stopped. "You know, you could get a dime or more for that."

"You really have no shame, Mamma, do you?" Essie yelled, no matter if it earned her face another backhand slap. "No shame!" Essie shut tight the carpetbag.

In three wide strides Mamma was beside her. She snatched the carpetbag from Essie's hands, threw it across the room. "Well, my dear girl, you go on out there and make your way!—have your new life!" She yanked the coral necklace from around Essie's neck.

The pitter-patter of the beads upon the floorboards brought mother and daughter to silence. For a tick of time both were transfixed by the *pitter-patter, pitter-patter.*

Essie saw a flash, not of anger, but of pain in Mamma's eyes.

Then the rage came roaring back. "Git!" she screamed. "Go right now—with just the clothes you got on your back!"

Essie was still frozen, feet stuck to the floor.

"Git!" Mamma yelled louder, "before I rip those clothes off you and toss you out naked like so much trash!"

Essie stumbled, almost tumbled down the attic steps. She was at the front door when Mamma cried out, "And you can tell your precious Clara Wiggins she don't work here no more!"

ASHES TO ASHES

Essie was pulled back from that slap when Reverend McElroy mumbled, "Ashes to ashes, dust to dust, looking for that blessed hope . . ."

The coffin was lowered into the ground.

Gravedigger Scriven handed her a shovel.

Essie managed half a shovelful of soil, tossed it onto the plain pine box.

"Thank you, Reverend," she softly said, pressing folded-up dollar bills into the minister's hand. She gave the grave-diggers a silver dollar each.

That done, with Binah and Ma Clara, Essie headed for Abby Bowfield's boardinghouse.

MY BONDAGE AND MY FREEDOM

Cook had a repast ready—cold capon, cucumber salad, potato salad, sweet tea with mint.

Essie had no appetite but she ate for Cook's sake.

"I best be getting home," said Ma Clara after about an hour and fanning herself. By the time they returned from Strangers' Ground the air was heavier, stickier. Breezes had ceased.

"I will see you before you go?" asked Ma Clara as Essie walked her to the front door, then out to the end of the walkway.

"You *know* you will." Essie planted a kiss on the old woman's cheek.

Back inside the boardinghouse, when Essie passed by the parlor, Abby Bowfield, tawny, stout, stern, called out for her.

"Yessum?"

Miss Abby was putting the final touches on an arrangement of camellias on the mahogany table in the center of the room. "I've spoken with Binah, told her it's fine if she helps you out tomorrow."

"Thank you, ma'am. I really appreciate that."

Essie looked around the parlor, wound back to her early days with the boardinghouse ways.

Set day for laundry, set day to clean the fireplaces, set day for window washing, set day for wiping down base-boards, door frames, doors. Set day for everything. Every day, twice a day, floors swept.

There were rules for the boarders too.

No drinking, except for a little scuppernong wine in the parlor Friday evenings.

No company in the bedrooms, only in the parlor for an hour and a half starting at eight o'clock in the evening. Except Sundays.

No company on Sundays.

Breakfast—seven o'clock sharp.

Supper—six o'clock sharp.

Nightly curfew—ten o'clock. Woe betide anyone who tried to enter the house at 10:02. She'd find herself locked out and in a scurry for a place to lay her head that night.

Overwhelmed by the rules at first, Essie soon eased into them, came to relish routine.

No folks coming in and out at strange hours, no noisy nights, no slamming doors, no cussing, no surprises, no shocks.

Nothing ever awry, haphazard. No one pared their toe-nails anywhere they pleased.

At Abby Bowfield's everything was aright. Like Essie had for so long wanted her life.

The boarders—teachers, seamstresses, live-out servants, a hairdresser, a midwife—a tidy lot. If a few gathered at eventide in the parlor, all was polite. Conversation calm. Laughter was titters and giggles, not guffaws. Sometimes the room was filled with just silence and scents of lilac and honeysuckle drifting in from the flower beds out front as the boarders read books, wrote letters, did petit point.

The parlor, with its gentle green camelback settee and matching side chairs, was Essie's favorite room. Its paw-footed mahogany bookshelf dearest. On its shelves, sixty-six books. Essie had counted them the first time she dusted that room.

"*The Scarlet Letter*," she said softly on the day she first scanned the titles. "*Clotel; or, the President's Daughter* . . . *The Mysterious Key and What It Opened* . . . *American Woman's Home* . . . *The Life and Public Services of Martin R. Delany* . . . *Forest Leaves* . . . *Great Expectations* . . . *My Bondage and My Freedom*." That last book was the most worn.

Essie was beside herself with joy when Miss Abby welcomed her to borrow books from the parlor. She hadn't been working there a week.

My Bondage and My Freedom was the book Essie took up to bed with her that very night.

* * *

Miss Abby was still fiddling with the camellias when Essie headed up to her room to change out of her mourning dress, then tackle chores double-time given how much of tomorrow she and Binah would be taking off to do a deed she sorely dreaded. But on the other side of it, Essie reminded herself, she'd be embarking on a new and wonderful life thanks to the woman who took Room #4.

PASSING STRANGE

"Them books along with the bookcase is from the woman who takes Room Number Four," Binah had told Essie one day while they were giving the parlor its weekly cleaning. "Had them shipped after one of her times passing through."

The parlor furniture was a gift from the woman too.

"After a different time," said Binah.

Room #4 was on the third floor of the east wing. It was a modest-sized room with waltz-out windows onto a balcony that overlooked a small courtyard dotted with potted palms and ferns. Creamy pink bougainvillea traipsed along the back gate.

"Parlor furniture Miss Abby had before was plenty nice but nowhere near as fancy," Binah had added as Essie polished the top of the center table and Binah its pedestal and paw feet.

Binah, a bit older than Essie, was the gentlest soul she

had ever met. Essie envied how she slept like the dead. Once her head hit the pillow Binah was out. No tossing and turning. No sleepless nights like Essie sometimes suffered.

"Let it be one you say is called a fairy tale," Binah often pleaded nights the girls weren't bone tired. Essie happily picked up the well-worn copy of Hans Christian Andersen's *Fairy Tales*, a book she'd bought at Miss Tansy's Odds-and-Ends Shop expressly for Binah, who often asked Essie to read the same story three nights in a row.

Essie always obliged, hoping it would spur Binah to want to learn to read. Within weeks of moving into Miss Abby's Essie had come to cherish Binah no matter that she was limited in conversation and prone to say strange things, was more like eight than eighteen. At least Essie had a friend. A sense of purpose too. There was so much that she could teach Binah, who had a peace about her Essie wished she had.

"Was left on Miss Abby's veranda in a sweetgrass basket, they say," Binah had casually told Essie. "Spose it was for the best." Sweet-tea-brown Binah, slack jawed and blind as a bat without her spectacles, had not a whit of curiosity about her ma or her pa. Neither did she mourn being born with a right arm a bit twisted and shorter than the left. "Makes me mighty grateful my each legs the same size," she said on one of the days the girls were out back with a bucket of steamed crabs. No, nothing much bothered Binah. She took everything in stride. Never took offense or got riled, not even when someone was cruel to her as happened one day when Cook sent them marketing.

Essie had been at Miss Abby's for just about a year on that bright May day when the girls walked arm in arm to the Market House. It teemed as ever with fruit peddlers, vegetable peddlers, butchers, fishmongers, women selling candy, selling flowers, vendors of every sort.

Binah was mesmerized by the great pile of corn in Miss Prichard's tiny stall, aiming to select ears with the most silk, Essie knew. Binah seemed to have her mind just about made up when a blowsy, snaggletoothed white woman yelled at her.

"Nigra, you is taking too long!" The woman shoved Binah aside so hard that she tumbled to the ground.

"I sorry," Binah responded to the woman, who never even glanced her way, just commenced dropping ear after ear of corn into her basket.

Just then a gang of white rowdies barreled through the crowd out to steal food and pickpocket like always. In the distance dogs sent up yelps and yaps.

Blood boiling, Essie helped Binah to her feet. "We can come back for the corn. Let's go get the squash."

The girls hadn't taken three steps when another commotion kicked up.

"What I done!? What I done!?" shouted a man, voice full of fear.

As she and Binah drew near, Essie saw that the frightened man was Primus Grady. Officer Riley McDermott, a churlish ox of a man chewing tobacco, was giving the old man a drubbing about the neck and head. Then he grabbed him by the arm.

"What I done!?" Primus Grady cried out again.

"I tole you, nigra, you can't be peddlin' chickens here without no license." The policeman released his grip, picked up the cage of chickens beside the old man's feet. The three scrawny bantams started squawking and running in circles.

Poor thing, thought Essie as she looked at the old man, bent and gaunt with a scraggly beard. Dirty homespun shirt kept closed with rusted safety pins. His patched pants, held up with a piece of cord, didn't even reach to his ankles. His run-down shoes lacked laces.

Cage in hand, Officer McDermott grabbed the old man's arm again. "You just earned yourself a twenty-dollar fine!"

"Sir," said Essie, pushing through the crowd. "Please, sir, Mister Grady, he's all he's got, barely scrapes by. Ain't no way he can pay a big fine."

Officer McDermott was red-faced. "You shut up!"

"Sir, I'm just—"

The policeman knocked Essie's market basket out of her

hands, shoved the cage of chickens at her, then snatched her up by the arm.

"Need help?" It was another policeman, Matthew Buckley, a man Essie used to call Uncle Matt.

Immediately Essie looked down at the ground.

"I got things under control," said the ox chewing tobacco.

"What's the charges?"

"This ole good-for-nothing ain't got no license. And this nigra wench was mouthin' off. Gonna charge her with disturbin' the peace."

Officer Buckley treated Essie to a wink and a roguish smile. "Riley, I know this gal. You can let her go."

Officer McDermott spat, released his grip on Essie. "If you say so, Matt, but if you ask me she need a good hidin'."

Avoiding Buckley's eyes, Essie grabbed her basket from the ground, hurried through the crowd and back to Binah.

Nearby stood Sarah Pace's prim and proper mother, Florence, with her sister, Drusilla. Both women were shaking their heads, looking prideful and disgusted.

Essie looked away.

"What a disgrace that Primus Grady is!" one snapped.

"Trash. Absolute trash!" said the other. And Essie could feel their eyes on her.

"Over three puny chickens," Essie muttered as she and Binah walked on. "You know what'll happen to Mister Grady if he can't pay that fine?"

"Policeman keep his chickens?"

The girls were nearing the Sheftall butcher's stall.

"They'll keep his chickens for sure. Also likely to make him work the fine off . . . Farm him out to some planter or put him on a chain gang doing road or railroad work." Essie had read of a colored woman who got ten years in the penitentiary for snatching five dollars from a white child's hand. "What white child goes about with five dollars?" Essie had scoffed after she read the item.

The girls were past Sheftall's stall, past a white graybeard peddling peacocks, past clusters of crates and barrels, when Essie sighed. "Will it ever end?"

"End? You mean the world?" asked Binah. She lit up. "Midwife Keziah say there be a book in the Bible that say the world will end one day. Yes, it will." Binah stopped, broke out into a broad smile. "Same book say there will be a new heaven and a new earth."

"I meant whitefolks ways, Binah. Like how that woman shoved you. How Officer McDermott troubled Primus Grady. You think he ever ask a white peddler if he has a license?"

Essie was steaming over other recent outrages. That white boy on Bull Street who shot a black boy in the leg for sassing him. She was also still galled over the Johnson C. Whittaker incident.

"At six o'clock yesterday," the *Savannah Morning News* had reported, "Johnson C. Whittaker, the colored cadet at West Point, was found in his room bound hand and foot, in a half-unconscious condition, and with a piece of one ear cut off." The paper later reported that the authorities believed Whittaker had mutilated himself, then made things look like he had been attacked.

"Even when we try to serve the nation . . . ," Essie mumbled. "Things going from bad to worse."

For the first time in a long time Essie thought about leaving Forest City. She had read about hundreds, thousands of Southern colored folks pulling up stakes, people called Exodusters, people seeking to get as far away as possible from places where colored were lynched, burned at the stake, beheaded, whipped, where colored women were constantly outraged, where whitefolks strutted around declaring, "This is a white man's country!"

"And all these doggone Confederate monuments they've been putting up," Essie muttered. Augusta. Thomasville. Macon. Quitman. Columbus. The *Savannah Morning News* celebrated the laying of cornerstones and unveilings of monuments outside of Georgia too. Essie had made a point to steer clear of Forsyth Park on the day the city replaced the statues of Justice and Silence atop its Confederate monument with a bronze statue of a Confederate soldier. As then so now Essie wished every one of the monuments struck by lightning as happened to the one in Lynchburg a few years back.

Essie had read that Kansas was the promised land for loads of Exodusters. Kansas, where land could be had for just a few dollars and where colored were free to build their own towns. Nicodemus was the first such town that came to mind on that bright May day at the Market House. Essie wondered what it would be like to live on the prairie, dwell in a sod house. Come winter could she bear up under the cold?

"End times!" Binah blurted out just as Essie ceased woolgathering about being an Exoduster. "That's what Midwife Keziah always say. End times!"

"Maybe she's right," said Essie, mind on how much ground colored had lost. "You know, Binah, there was a time, back after slavery days, we had colored men on the city council, also in the state legislature. Was a time we had about a dozen colored man in the US Congress. One was from Georgia. Jefferson Long . . . Now I think we don't have but one, Senator Blanche K. Bruce of Mississippi."

"What did those colored men do?"

"Make laws, run things . . . You know here in Savannah we had our own colored fire companies, but they broke them up a few years back."

Binah frowned. "Where's the harm in colored men putting out a fire?"

Essie shook her head. "Whitefolks want all the power."

"What make them like that?"

Essie shrugged.

"Think when come the new heaven and the new earth whitefolks will learn to share?"

"I don't know, Binah," Essie replied. "I just don't know. It's passing strange."

FINDINGS

Only complaint Essie had about Binah was how she junked up the top-floor room they shared, junked it up with stacks of crates containing her "findings."

"Could mean somethin' to somebody," Binah usually said when Essie asked, "Now, Binah, what in the world are you going to do with *that?*"

That might have been an empty blue ink bottle, a tortoiseshell hair comb missing most of its teeth, a couple of wooden alphabet blocks. Thrown-away things. Things Binah found in the street or in boarders' waste bins.

When the spirit moved her Binah filled a bushel basket with findings and lugged it over to washerwoman Hetty Denegal's cottage on Bay Street. Miss Hetty mothered stray children, some true orphans, others half orphans with their one living parent in prison, in the asylum, or just run off.

A wooden and papier-mâché doll with a missing leg

topped the basket Binah toted to Bay Street on the day Miss Abby told them the news: "You two will soon need to ready Room Number Four. She will be here in two weeks."

"You know, Binah, I never even asked you her name," Essie said as they cleaned the kitchen that night.

"Whose name?"

"Room Number Four."

"Dorcas Vashon."

"Dorcas . . . Vashon," Essie repeated. "Will we need to do anything out of the ordinary in readying her room?"

Binah shook her head. "Just make sure we don't forget to put a mosquito net on her bedposts. One time I forgot and Miss Abby got mighty cross."

"What's she like, Dorcas Vashon?" Essie asked the next day as she and Binah sat at the big wooden worktable in the kitchen. Essie stringing and snapping green beans. Binah shucking corn.

"Nice. Keep to herself though," replied Binah.

Binah being Binah, Essie knew she would batch up the cornsilk for drying, bundle up the husks, and in a few days' time start making dolls for the Bay Street strays.

"How often does this Dorcas Vashon come?" asked Essie.

"One year she came once. Another year twice. I can't remember all her comings."

"For how long does she stay?"

"Days. Maybe a week or more."

"Where's she from?"

Binah shrugged, then smiled. "Carolina. Charleston, I believe."

"Why Miss Abby don't rent the room out to other people in Dorcas Vashon's absence?"

Binah looked around. There was no one else in the kitchen but them. Still, Binah lowered her voice. "Miss Dorcas don't want no other spirits in that room. She pay Miss Abby a tidy sum for it to be that way."

Essie was convinced that Binah was making that up.

Then again what else could explain such a waste of money? Unless paying for a room she wasn't all the time using was just another way of being generous.

"Must be a very rich woman," Essie said as she sat there stringing and snapping. Not in the *Savannah Morning News*, not in the *Tribune* had Essie ever read of a colored woman like Dorcas Vashon.

"Rich she is for sure," said Binah, "but don't nobody know where the richness come from." Again Binah looked around the kitchen. "But there is whispers."

"Whispers?"

"One is that she put a hex on a white man to make him leave her his big ole house in New Orleans—or maybe it was in Charleston. I disremember." Binah paused. "Besides that big house, there was other property. That whisper I heard from Patty."

"Patty who was here before me?"

Binah nodded, pushed her glasses up her nose. "Trunk-ful of gold, too, if you ask me."

"Trunkful of gold?" Essie was confused.

Binah nodded. "I bet that white man she hexed had a big ole trunk of gold."

Essie tried not to laugh.

Binah leaned in. "I heard Cook say onliest way a colored woman could have so much money was if she ran houses of illput."

"Houses of what?"

"Illput."

"You mean ill-repute?"

Binah nodded. "That sound more like it." She pushed her spectacles up her nose again. "What kind of place is that, Essie?"

Essie thought for a bit. "It's a place—well, like my ma's place."

When the girls were first getting to know each other, Essie had told Binah that she left home because it was rowdy, like a boardinghouse where people could kick up a ruckus all times of day and night.

Essie had strung and snapped three pounds of beans. One more pound to go.

And she counted the days before she'd meet the myste-rious Dorcas Vashon. She couldn't wait!

EYES AFIRE

Essie was wiping down the rockers on the veranda when a jet-black carriage pulled up. She looked to the street seconds before the driver's "Whoa."

She put down the rag, straightened her dress, smoothed her hair at the sides, then dashed down the walkway. She beat the driver to the carriage door, freeing him up to tend to just the luggage.

"Miss Dorcas Vashon?" Essie asked as chipper as she could. She opened the carriage door, offered an arm.

"Yes, my dear, I am."

"Name's Essie, ma'am." Essie was surprised, disappointed actually, that Dorcas Vashon's high-neck black dress was so plain. Not a bit of lace or beading on the collar or cuffs. No ribbon work. Essie had envisioned her arriving in something very fancy.

But the woman was just as Binah had described her. "Short, thin-boned, crinkly hair, a tad darker than you.

Always wears black. Likes to take her meals in her room. And she don't eat meat." However, Binah had said nothing about the elfin woman's eyes.

Eyes afire.

Could burn a hole through a rock.

Once Essie settled Dorcas Vashon into Room #4, she fetched her a glass of sweet tea, asked if there was anything else she could do for her. All the while Essie kept her head lowered in fear of those eyes.

"No, my dear. I will just rest awhile."

Essie curtsied, began to back out of the room.

"My dear, please tell Cook that I will take supper at seven," said Dorcas Vashon.

Essie had just reached the doorway.

"Yessum." Essie made a mental note. Apparently Dorcas Vashon could take her meals anytime she pleased.

Earlier in the week Essie had several times practiced carrying a tray laden with food up to Room #4. She practiced again the day Dorcas Vashon arrived. Still, when Cook placed the plate of roasted vegetables, a bowl of lentil soup, and a glass of lemonade on the silver plate tray, Essie was a featherhead.

She was almost through the kitchen door when she panicked.

Can't hold the tray and knock at the same time.

She hadn't thought to practice that.

Essie turned around. "Binah, come with me, please."

Binah put down the dish she was washing, dried her hands.

"You walk ahead of me, do the knocking," said Essie.

A few days later, when Essie was in Room #4 to take away the supper tray and ask Dorcas Vashon if she needed anything—

"Sit with me awhile," the woman replied. "That is if it won't keep you from your duties."

"It won't, ma'am," said Essie. Even if it meant that she didn't get all her chores done until after midnight, Essie was not about to say no to Dorcas Vashon.

WINDLESS, FIREFLY NIGHT

Essie took to rising at five o'clock instead of five thirty so that she could get an earlier start on work. For Dorcas Vashon, again and again, bade her to visit with her for a while.

"How long have you been working here, Essie?" the woman asked on one occasion when Essie was tidying Room #4.

"Going on two years."

"Were you born in Savannah?"

"Yessum."

"Was your family born in Savannah?" That question came on another day.

Essie bit her lip. "I don't know anything about my pa, ma'am. My ma, she came here on Sherman's March."

"From where?"

Essie shrugged. "Never said."

"Is your mother still alive?"

"Yessum."

"Do you spend your day off with her?"

Essie swallowed. "No, ma'am. We had a falling-out."

"Over what?"

Essie squirmed. "If you don't mind, ma'am, I'd rather not say."

"I see."

Essie wondered how much the woman saw, really *saw*.

"What are your plans?" asked Dorcas Vashon the following day.

Essie had just brought in a vase of hydrangeas fresh cut from the front yard.

"Plans?"

"What kind of future do you want? You strike me as someone who wants to make something of herself."

"Thank you, ma'am."

Was the woman a mind reader?

Essie had recently been daydreaming about saving up enough money to leave Savannah, make her way to one of the schools that trained up colored teachers. When done, she'd create a special school that would also be a home for children tossed aside, forced to fend for themselves, hope for mercies. *I will lavish them with love*, Essie vowed when she dreamed of her home for kicked-aside kids.

"And I'll teach them that it makes no never mind how

a body starts out in life. It matters that you reach for something, elevate, exalt yourself."

Essie let those words tumble out on the night that she
and Dorcas Vashon were standing on Room #4's balcony,
its high black cast-iron railing an arabesque of ivy.
Months back Miss Abby had the balconies along with the
back gate redone by a man who lived a solitary life on the
outskirts of town, a man who intrigued Essie with his quiet
ways and sad eyes. Whenever he did work for a colored
person he always gave a discount Binah had told her.

"They say Mister Caleb the best blacksmith for a hundred miles," Binah had also said. Like Ma Clara he was
beautifully black and carried himself as if a prince or king
in another life. Essie wondered why such a nice, successful, handsome man wasn't married as she stood on his won-
drously wrought balcony with Dorcas Vashon.

It was a windless night. Fireflies played hide-and-seek
in the courtyard below.

By then Essie no longer feared Dorcas Vashon's eyes.
During their chats she had spied in those fiery eyes mercy,
compassion, comfort. A time or two Essie had wanted to tell
Dorcas Vashon why she left that house on Minis Street,
tell her the truth about Mamma, but in the end she backed
down, fearing that the woman might spurn her.

"You have nothing to be ashamed about," said Dorcas
Vashon out of the blue one morning. "There is no place for
shame in your life."

Had Miss Abby told her? Had she hired a private detective? Was she even talking about Mamma? Or just about her being a poor drudge? Essie dared not ask.

It was a few days later, on that windless, firefly night that Dorcas Vashon made Essie an offer.

OF PROMISE

"I can take you from this place and give you a different life."

"Different life?"

"A better life."

"How would you do that?"

"Turn you into a lady, help you rise in life."

"But how come—why would you do that for me?"

"It is what I do. I seek out young women of promise."

"But—but why?"

"I have had blessings abundant, my dear. And so many of our people are in such great need. Ever since they hammered the final nail in Reconstruction's coffin back in '77 . . ." Dorcas Vashon paused, shook her head. "So many fail to rise not on account of a lack of ambition, but on account of a lack of opportunity, a chance."

Essie saw that the concern, the grief were genuine.

"In any event, I aid as many of our institutions as

I can, places like the school a young man named Booker T. Washington will soon open in Tuskegee, Alabama. Along with institutions, I invest in individuals, especially young women who can use a helping hand."

Essie was still taking it all in. "You truly believe that I can . . ."

"Yes, I do, my dear."

The fireflies were more numerous, enchanting the night.

"If you decide to accept my offer," Dorcas Vashon continued, "your journey will begin in Baltimore. And you should know, my dear, that it will not be easy."

Essie nodded rapidly, both elated and terrified.

"But I do believe in my bones, Essie, that you can meet the challenge, that you can be transformed, that you can rise to higher heights. Once there you will, you must, give others a helping hand."

What if the whispers were true? What if she had put a hex on a man? What if she did own houses of—?

"Sleep on it," said Dorcas Vashon as she turned to leave the balcony. "No rush. Spend some time on self-reflection. Decide if you can leave all of this behind, cut all ties, and enter a new life."

I want my own life, Mamma—a better *life, a* new *life!*

Was Dorcas Vashon dangerous or the answer to prayer?

Essie lingered on the balcony a little longer, eyes on the flickering of fireflies in the courtyard below.

WANTED

Essie told Binah about the offer that night. Rattling on so, it was a while before she realized that Binah had dozed off.

Pacing in the narrow space between their beds, Essie imagined a fine future as a lady: walking stately along a promenade with parasol and wide-brimmed hat . . . sailing on a placid lake . . . attending a banquet, a ball.

What was that bubbly drink rich people enjoyed in a . . . ? *Flute.*

That was the word. Champagne flute. Essie had long ago vowed to never let a drop of whiskey touch her tongue, but champagne, that was different. She never read of champagne turning people ugly.

Most of all, as Essie thought hard about Dorcas Vashon's offer, she imagined a life without shame.

How could she rise, elevate where she was? She would never be allowed into Savannah's colored society. People like the Paces, the Deveauxs, the Coopers, people who were members of the Ladies and Gents Club or the Union Coterie, clubs that had fancy dinners and balls—such people would never cotton to the company of the likes of her, would never welcome her to their picnics and steamboat rides. What damning looks she had gotten a while back when she went to one of their churches in her very best frock, shoes shined, not a hair out of place. She had even purchased a new bonnet. Did they not know that she no longer had anything to do with that house on Minis Street? Could they not see that she was *nothing* like her mother? Attending the praise house on Shad Island eased some of the sting. Nobody looked down on her there.

If she stayed in Savannah . . .

Grow old at Miss Abby's?

End up with aching ankles, stiff knees. Nothing to look forward to but lovage and lavender foot soaks?

Anytime Essie skimmed the WANTED column in the *Savannah Morning News* there were only lowly jobs for colored.

"Wanted, a competent colored house girl . . ."

"Wanted, a colored girl for chamber work and plain sewing . . ."

"Wanted, reliable colored girl as maid . . ."

When Essie awoke the next morning to predawn light, larksong, and a milkman's bell, she pictured herself holding her head up high. Saw herself married to a wonderful man, someone of stature. They'd have children, children she'd love with all her mind, heart, soul. All her being.

She began to tear up.

Essie moved through the day—dusting, sweeping, mopping, other chores—in a trance and with doubts nipping at her dreams.

Could she really go off to Baltimore with a woman who was still so very much a stranger? All Essie knew about Dorcas Vashon was that she preferred lemonade to sweet tea, loved succotash, and liked her eggs scrambled soft. True, she no longer feared the woman's eyes, but every now and then she glimpsed a bit of mischief in them, something impish.

Baltimore? The Monumental City.

Hope surged.

Until Essie remembered that Baltimore was also called Mob Town.

Frederick Douglass. He had spent some of his slavery days in Baltimore. It's where, in a shipyard, a bunch of white boys, apprentices like him, beat him up for no reason and almost knocked an eye out.

Essie was about to tackle polishing brass, doorknobs to push plates, when she thought better of Baltimore. It was, after all, where Frederick Douglass began trying to better himself. And he was a slave!

Maybe Baltimore *was* the place for her.

AS BRAVE AS FREDERICK
DOUGLASS?

The next night, for the second time, Essie took up to bed with her Frederick Douglass's autobiography *My Bondage and My Freedom*. Against the backdrop of Binah's snores, she turned to a favorite passage.

"Seized with a determination to learn to read, at any cost, I hit upon many expedients to accomplish the desired end. The plea which I mainly adopted, and the one by which I was most successful, was that of using my young white playmates, with whom I met in the street, as teachers. I used to carry, almost constantly, a copy of Webster's spelling book in my pocket; and, when sent on errands, or when play time was allowed me, I would step, with my young friends, aside, and take a lesson in spelling."

He had paid for his lessons with bits of bread. Essie wondered if that meant at times he went hungry. She read on.

"When I was about thirteen years old, and had succeeded in learning to read, every increase of knowledge, especially respecting the FREE STATES, added something to the almost intolerable burden of the thought—'I AM A SLAVE FOR LIFE.' To my bondage I saw no end. It was a terrible reality, and I shall never be able to tell how sadly that thought chafed my young spirit."

But he didn't remain in despair! That was the important thing.

Essie closed the book, tucked it under her chin. She thought about how young Douglass managed to squirrel away fifty cents from shining shoes to buy another book, *The Columbian Orator.* Essie pictured him reading that book again and again. The way he talked about that book it was only second to the Bible.

Freedom was his dream and he never let it go! Essie put the book beneath her pillow, blew out the candle. She knew better than to compare her life with that of a slave's, knew what a blessing it was to be free. But she couldn't deny feeling chained, bound, held back from rising in life because of who brought her into the world.

Wanted, a competent colored house girl...

As she lay there, enveloped by the pitch-black night with whip-poor-wills calling, with breezes bustling, rustling through live oaks, magnolias, river birches, sugar maples,

Essie thought about how Frederick Douglass hadn't known what to expect when he finally reached New York City.

Could she be as brave as Frederick Douglass?

He was a grown man when he took his liberty.

She was sixteen.

She remembered, too, that after his initial jubilee over finally being *free*, Frederick Douglass was awfully scared. Sleeping in the streets. Surviving on crusts of bread. Friendless. Utterly alone until someone, thank goodness, steered him to a colored man who could help him.

And look at him now! The most famous colored man in the country, in the world. Went from the slave Frederick Bailey to the gentleman Frederick Douglass!

Maybe she didn't even have to be as brave as Frederick Douglass. Her journey was different.

She wasn't escaping slavery.

She wouldn't be making her way alone, but traveling with the wealthy Dorcas Vashon.

Between sleep and wake Essie hit upon the one thing that would help her make up her final mind.

BISCUITS AND VERBENA TEA

"If you don't mind, ma'am, there's someone I'd like you to meet." Essie had just set down the breakfast tray.

"And who would that be?" asked Dorcas Vashon, still with a bit of sleep in her eyes.

"Ma—Clara Wiggins, who used to clean for my ma, someone who's been like a mother to me."

Essie sat outside Room #4 while the two women talked over biscuits and verbena tea. She was as squirmy as she had been years earlier when she peered into Mamma's red room from behind Ma Clara's skirt, praying for that yes to school.

BLESSED, TRULY BLESSED

"What do you think?" Essie asked Ma Clara as the two stood on Abby Bowfield's veranda. Essie couldn't keep still, couldn't stop wringing her hands, couldn't keep her eyes from darting every which way.

What if Ma Clara advised against it?

What if she knew a whisper about Dorcas Vashon to be true?

But then Ma Clara smiled. "I think you have found favor with a good soul," the old woman finally said. "You have been blessed, truly blessed."

"So I should say yes to the offer?"

"Chance of a lifetime, sweetness."

"Really? You really mean it?" Essie rubbed her hands together.

"Mean it?" Ma Clara balled up both fists. "Anybody try to keep you from this opportunity I'll knock 'em headlong into tomorrow."

Essie hugged Ma Clara—"Thank you! Thank you!"—
then dashed back into the house, bounded up the stairs,
flew into Room #4.

Breathless, she just stood in the doorway, too over-
joyed, too overwhelmed to speak.

Dorcas Vashon smiled. "Shall I take this as a yes?"

That evening Dorcas Vashon asked three of the seamstresses
at Abby Bowfield's to make Essie several smart outfits.
"Something in daffodil . . . Something in heliotrope . . ."
Dorcas Vashon gave the women instructions as they
took Essie's measurements.

"We will leave in two weeks," Dorcas Vashon informed
Essie.

A few days later . . .

TOMORROW

"They say your ma is doing poorly. Can't fend for herself much."

A roll of thunder rattled the sky.

Ma Clara had just sat down at the kitchen worktable.

Essie fetched her a glass of water.

Nearly two years had elapsed since Essie laid eyes on Mamma. After she said "Yes!" to Dorcas Vashon's offer Essie had been in knots over whether or not to tell Mamma that she was leaving Forest City. She feared it would only foment more friction, feared Mamma hurling nasty words at her again.

"Seems she has been sending the Rakestraw boy mostly to fetch her food and such," said Ma Clara after a sip of water.

Essie furrowed her brow. "But what about Miss Emma and Miss Katy? Can't they—"

"Lit out."

Days later Ma Clara returned. "I check on her as I can. Take soup. She sent for Doctor Buzzard, and he's been treating her with roots and his crazy potions. Put some chicken-bone-and-feather charm about her neck."

Essie was afraid to ask.

After a heavy silence Ma Clara took Essie's hands in hers. "It's the waste-away, sweetness."

Essie swallowed, stared down at the clinker-brick floor. She had reckoned that Mamma was just having a long sick headache or maybe was just a bit bilious. She figured Katy and Emma left because they'd found a better house out of which to ply their trade. "I'll look in on her tomorrow," she said.

Tomorrow became tomorrow became . . . Ma Clara coming with the news that Essie was out of tomorrows . . . became Dorcas Vashon insisting on paying for the undertaker, the funeral, buying her that magnificent black mourning dress.

Essie gasped and her hands flew to her face when Dorcas Vashon held the dress before her.

The woman then flooded her with its details. "It is a silk faille floor-length dress, long-sleeved, fitted bodice with off-white tatted lace trim at the neck and at the end of the sleeves."

Faille? Tatted lace? Bodice? Not words Essie knew. She

just stood there in Room #4, mouth agape, feeling like a Cinderella, a dazed Cinderella at that. More so as Dorcas Vashon continued.

"The lower portion of the dress flows into a full silhouette, which features black satin and . . ."

Essie couldn't keep up with the words.

". . . chevron-shaped pleats and rows of embroidered wide-edged black beaded fringe on the front." Dorcas Vashon twirled the dress around.

Essie smiled at the sight of the modest train that was—

"What we have here, my dear, is a maze of tucks, pleats, ruffles, and inserts of black moiré and satin piping." Dorcas Vashon finished with this: "The entire dress is embellished with bugle-beaded corded appliqués."

All those words for one dress? Essie felt utterly unworthy, guilty too for being so happy. She was about to bury her mother. How could she take such delight in a dress?

Essie looked from the dress to Dorcas Vashon. "I don't know what to say. Bless your heart, Miss Dorcas."

Three days later Essie stood in Strangers' Ground with Binah, Ma Clara, Gravedigger Bogins, Gravedigger Scriven, and Reverend Zephaniah McElroy.

And with the past snatching her back.

MA SOMETHIN'

The morning after Mamma was laid under the earth, Essie and Binah left Miss Abby's following breakfast. Both wore ratty half aprons over dingy dresses and old boots, had faded kerchiefs on their heads. They carried buckets, scrub brushes, brooms, carpet beaters. The sack over Essie's shoulder bulged with soap, lime, sweet oil, and other cleaning supplies. Binah's was stuffed with rags.

Turning off Bryan, they made a right onto Broad, walked south, both girls with the same wide stride.

"Hello there, Essie, Binah," called out Old Man Boney. He was riding by in the larger of his carts, loaded with lumber and hitched to his stoutest ox, humpbacked Jake with an unusually long dewlap.

"Hey, there, Old Man Boney!" the girls said in unison.

"Hello there, girls!" Old Man Boney bade Jake take it slow, then gave Essie a long look. "You look like you about to some way, somehow do us proud, Essie."

How does he know? Like her, Binah and Ma Clara had been sworn to secrecy. Essie wasn't sure how much Miss Abby knew. Spooked, Essie finally said, "I'll sure try, sir."

With a gentle tap of a horsetail rush Old Man Boney bade Jake to speed up.

Essie had a bit more bounce in her step. Mind on her future and off the grim task ahead, she waxed happy over the gardens they passed. Rings of marigolds or petunias or sunflowers—or a mix—bordered by oyster shells or stones. Clusters of oleander bushes. One front yard had nothing but daisies, another luscious lilac hydrangeas.

"When the new girl start?" Binah asked during a stretch of shade thanks to pines.

"Day I leave."

"Her name again?"

"Betty."

"That's right, she start with a *b* like me. Binah and Betty . . . Betty and Binah . . ."

Essie made a mental note to tell Betty to be extra kind to Binah.

"She seemed nice when she came the other day." Binah paused. "Can she read?"

"Don't know," replied Essie. "But you can sure ask her when she comes for training on Saturday."

Essie was daydreaming of a splendid garden in her future when she realized Binah was no longer by her side. She looked back.

Binah was huddled beneath a bay tree as if seeking

shelter from a storm. The look on her face wasn't quite worry, wasn't quite fear.

"Binah, what's wrong?"

Binah hung her head. "Been itchin' to ask you . . ."

"What is it, Binah?" Essie thought one of her worst fears was upon her. What if Binah wanted to come with her to Baltimore? How could she tell her that Dorcas Vashon was not interested in her, didn't see in her a young woman of promise?

Binah gave Essie a sidelong glance.

"Binah, what is it?" Essie nudged again.

"Well, it's . . . I been wonderin' now that you got a new fairy godmother in Miss Dorcas, if I—if maybe I can have Miss Clara for mine."

Essie was so relieved. "I'm sure she wouldn't mind, Binah, not at all."

"Think she will allow for me to call her Ma Clara?"

Miss Abby had been good to Binah, but she was not a warm woman, didn't have Ma Clara's heart. "I'm sure she won't mind one bit," said Essie.

Binah brightened. "Nice to have someone to call Ma somethin'."

As the girls walked on, Essie eased back to past saunters around Forest City, to her long stares at mansions, imagining what it would be like to live in a big fancy house.

Like haunting Green Mansion on Madison Square. Pretty soft pink walls and all that fanciful ironwork . . .

Like the brick and brownstone Davenport House on State Street, a soaring house with a wrought-iron double-entry stairway . . .

When she passed by the fountain in Forsyth Park she used to toss in an imaginary penny and whisper a wish for a better life.

The girls had just passed Liberty Street when Essie let herself dream about the wonders she'd find in Dorcas Vashon's home in Baltimore.

GONE

Queasy. A touch faint. That was Essie entering the house on Minis Street. It smelled like death and horror.

She headed for the spittoon near the piano, made it a doorstop, then had Binah follow her into the kitchen. "Any food in the larder, throw it out. I'm going around back to make a fire."

Fire pit alive with licking, hungry flames, Essie headed for the house. Along the way, she grabbed a large galvanized tub that sat upside down on the porch. Once inside, she had Binah follow her upstairs.

Essie's face fell when she stepped into what had been Emma's room with its loud green wallpaper, a jamboree of purple petunias.

No bedclothes. No pillows, rug, curtains, kerosene lamp, wall sconces, pitcher and bowl from the washstand, candlestick holders that used to sit on the mantel . . . Gone.

Everything but the bedstead, chest of drawers, dressing table, nightstand.

Maybe it wasn't Emma. Perhaps a neighbor.

Katy's room, with its bright-pink wallpaper, had been looted too. Would she find the same thing in the third bedroom? Essie took a deep breath before opening that door.

"Goodness, what a fancy room!" Binah exclaimed.

Essie hurried to open the window. "Strip the bed, will you, please, then take down the curtains. Dump it all on the back porch." Essie didn't want Binah near the fire pit by herself.

While Binah did her part, Essie tackled the dresser drawers, dumped clothing—underthings, stockings, blouses—into the tin tub.

Next, the wardrobe. Dresses, skirts, robes, shoes—into the tin tub.

When Binah went downstairs with her lot, Essie reached under the bed, removed a floorboard, brought out a cigar box.

A gold flower-shaped ring with a cluster of diamonds around a stone the color of whiskey . . . gold necklace . . . pearl necklace . . . earbobs like tiny chandeliers . . . bank notes. That's what Essie remembered seeing inside the cigar box years ago.

All gone. Like the dressing table's silver vanity set—comb, brush, hand mirror, powder jar, rouge pots.

Essie remembered another hiding place. She reached

behind the chest of drawers, felt around for an old hemp drawstring bag taped to the back. Found it. Brought it up. When she looked inside—

Pitter-patter, pitter-patter.

She counted them.

Twenty-two coral beads.

Essie was shocked, perplexed.

Why had Mamma kept them?

Did it mean that she—?

"Get ahold of yourself," Essie whispered. She put the beads in a pocket. She tossed the cigar box, the hemp bag into the tin tub.

A blouse, a robe, a dress.

"Why you burnin' them clothes?" Binah cried out, shuttering like a leaf. Essie had never seen Binah so upset. "They could mean somethin'—"

"No one would want any of it. Shot through with sickness," Essie replied. "And so much sin," she added under her breath.

"Can't give it all a good wash?"

"No." Essie dumped the rest of what was in the tub into the fire.

Binah shrank back to the porch, where she stood biting her fingernails, shaking her head.

As fire reduced Mamma's things to ashes, Essie couldn't

turn from the flames. She willed them to burn away every foul, filthy memory.

Of that closet in the room on Factors Row.

Of sordid goings-on in that Minis Street house.

Of being dragged, when little, to fortune-teller Madam Smith on York near Whitaker, where she was made to sit in a dark, smelly corner of a room while the grotesque Madam Smith, with her purple turban, flowing red robe, and corncob pipe, read palms or peered into tea leaves, then mumbled things. So embarrassing how loud Mamma and the aunties cackled about the grand lives they'd have as they sashayed out of Madam Smith's.

"Binah, bring on the bedclothes and curtains." Essie didn't even look over her shoulder.

"You burning them too? You might could just—"

Essie spun around. "Binah! Please, just do as I ask!"

Binah obliged without a peep.

"Thank you, Binah, and I'm sorry for yelling at you. I—"

"It didn't hurt that bad, Essie. Just a finger prick. Besides, I know you got burdens on you."

Guilt ridden, Essie wondered if she'd ever be as forgiving as Binah. "I just didn't know that this would be so . . . so hard."

"I say you too hard on yourself, Essie."

How Essie would miss Binah's grace, her calm.

Billows of smoke conjured up times she had dropped to her knees, prayed for Mamma to change her ways just as Ma Clara had told her to do.

"You see, as I heard it, she had a terrible coming up. In slavery her whitefolks abused her every which way, left her broken in mind. Because of things they made her do, your ma came to believe she had no talent for nothing except, well . . ." That was the sort of thing Ma Clara used to tell Essie.

All that praying, all that pleading . . .

She had stopped praying for Mamma years ago, after the summer yellow jack struck and Mamma reached death's door.

"My Essie . . . ?" Mamma cried out as Ma Clara nursed her with quinine and mustard plasters. "Where my Essie . . . My Essie, she fine? . . . Tell her I said I love her. She all I ever had."

And the way Mamma called out to God, promising hard to change her ways if she lived. Then she rallied right around the time the fever left Forest City. By Christmas uncles were once again trooping in and out of that house on Minis Street.

THREE CORAL BEADS

Essie left the attic for last.

"Used to be my room," she told Binah as she brought the ladder down.

Essie was shocked once up there.

The room wasn't done up in red. It was exactly as she had left it except for the missing bedclothes, kerosene lamp, pitcher and face bowl, and other small features.

Essie wiped a finger across the highboy. Two years of dust. She opened the window, looked around the room. In a dark corner down by the baseboard she spotted three coral beads. Picking them up, she felt a bit faint.

"What's wrong?" asked Binah.

"From a necklace I had," Essie muttered. "Birthday gift. I was nine."

"From your ma?"

Essie nodded, pulled back to that day in Miss Viola's

dress shop on Liberty Street. Essie had spied the necklace in the shop's window.

"Oooh, that's so pretty!" she gasped, pointing the necklace out to Mamma.

"Uh-huh," Mamma grunted, then went back to choosing fabric.

A few weeks later Mamma surprised Essie with the necklace.

"Used to hear old folks say coral keep you from harm," said Mamma as she put the necklace around Essie's neck.

Rocking horse . . . ball and stick . . . limberjack . . . pocket doll . . . whistle. Random gifts over the years. Nothing as precious as the necklace. Never before had Mamma paid her such close attention. Never before had Essie seen such tenderness in her eyes as when she surprised her with that necklace.

"What happened to the rest of them beads—what happened to the whole neckpiece?" asked Binah.

"Broke."

"How it broke?"

"An accident."

"Couldn't be remedied?"

"It's a long story, Binah."

Essie stepped over to the small wall shelf, removed the books and magazines, laid them on the bed, then took the wall shelf down. "My prized possession." She smiled. "First big purchase. Bought it from Miss Tansy's. Twenty cents, I think. Five, six years ago." Essie frowned. "It was red. Scared up some blue paint and a brush." Essie had wanted only gentle colors in her life, colors like mint green, pale yellow, and what she called blue-sky blue, which she also used to paint her window frame.

Money for the wall shelf came from change Mamma sometimes tossed her way and coins she got from Katy and Emma for running errands.

"Git me some Old Baker Whiskey."

"Go be on the lookout for she-crab women and get me a dozen."

"Run and go git me a tin of snuff."

"Need a bottle of Old Carolina Bitters."

"Run over to Nolan's on Bryan for a quart of oysters."

Essie had also earned money from Ma Clara, for helping her clean homes some days.

Essie handed the bookshelf to Binah. "I want you to have it. The books, magazines too."

"But I can't—"

"But you *can learn*, Binah, and you *should* learn. Promise me you will." Arms akimbo, Essie scanned the books and magazines. "Before the shelf came these. I used to like nothing better than to go to Miss Tansy's shop and pick through books and magazines her daughter found in the trash when cleaning for whitefolks."

Essie whispered the titles. "*The Raven . . . Great*

Expectations... My favorites were *A Christmas Carol* and *Oliver Twist.*"

"Fairy tales?" Binah was beaming.

"Almost," replied Essie. "In one an ornery old man with more money that he knows what to do with becomes like a godfather to a crippled boy. In the other, a vagabond orphan thief ends up with a princely life. Those stories kept me hoping that a miracle would come my way."

"Jesus-like miracles? Feed a whole mess of folks with just two fishes and a few loafs?"

Essie laughed. "Like what Dorcas Vashon is doing for me."

Essie picked up an 1873 issue of *Oliver Optic's Magazine, Our Boys and Girls.* She turned the pages until she came to—

"'The Youth of Queen Victoria.'" She glanced up at Binah. "I must've read this story a hundred and one times."

"Another almost fairy tale?"

"No, not at all. When she was little Queen Victoria didn't have a very happy life. Her father died when she was a baby young. She spent a lot of time alone as a child. No friends. Like me."

Binah went wide-eyed. "But I'm your friend."

"I mean before, when I lived in this house."

Seeing as how she hadn't told Binah the truth about Mamma, Essie couldn't very well now tell her about her days at Beach Institute where it had been impossible for her to have friends because Sarah Pace constantly called her gutter girl, chanted "Essie is messy!" even when she wasn't.

Then came the day when during recess Sarah Pace walked up to her, stuck out her tongue, and shouted, "Your ma is a—"

The word burned like acid. Hot tears lined Essie's face. "She's not!" she shouted, then shoved Sarah Pace with all her might.

"She's too!" whimpered Sarah Pace from down on the ground.

"She's not!" Essie shouted again, then ran to the other side of the yard, plopped down by the fence, and cried herself a river.

Shunned. Teased. Some boys tried to drag Essie behind the school or into the bushes, whispering, "I'll give you candy."

"Get off me!" Essie screamed that day Michael Mack grabbed her by one arm, Jimmy Mason by the other. Thank goodness Miss Purdy heard her cries and came racing from the building with ruler in hand.

Your ma is a—!

Essie had given up school, it got so bad.

"I will teach myself," she had vowed, made up her mind to forgo candy, whirligigs, and whatnot and save whatever money she came by for trips to Miss Tansy's Odds-and-Ends Shop for books, magazines, and half-used copybooks so that she could practice her penmanship. It's why she never tossed a real penny into the fountain in Forsyth Park.

Reading was her second rescue, second refuge. Out back in the arbor covered in yellow jessamines on balmy days, cuddled up in the attic on days of chill or rain. Caught up in a story she shut out the chaos.

But not always, like the day Emma cussed out Katy for using up her rouge.

"Youse a liar!" yelled Katy.

"You step foot in my room one more time and I will cut you to ribbons!" Emma threatened.

"If you think—"

"Both y'all shut up!" Mamma shouted. "Tole y'all I got a sick headache."

No friends to be had on Minis Street. The few girls around her age gave her odd looks, steered clear, just as she avoided Alston Rakestraw, a bookbinder's apprentice. His leers made her tremble.

"Before you, Binah, my only friends were these books and magazines—and the *Tribune*, a colored paper that used to be put out right here in Savannah. Owned and operated by John H. Deveaux, who lives on Duffy near Habersham, the one who has that important job at the Customs House."

Binah squinted as she often did when trying to remember something.

"Anyway, you should have seen Ma Clara when she showed me that first issue. Beside herself with pride."

Pride was exactly what Essie had felt as she read that first issue: Saturday, December 4, 1875. The whole front page was devoted to a sermon by a Reverend H. M. Turner. He took as his title "Thou God Seest Me." It was from a Bible story about a woman thrust out into a wilderness without a crust of bread. But God kept watch over this woman.

"Thou God seest me," Essie whispered as she read the rest of Turner's sermon. "Thou God seest me." She also remembered how she puzzled over the words "elevation" and "exalt," then figured out that they had to do with reaching for higher heights, having a better life.

The hunger of her heart.

Thou God seest me.

"You used to read that paper like how you now read the white paper?" asked Binah.

"Oh yes! After Ma Clara finished an issue she passed it on to me. I learned so much from the *Tribune.* Like about how all over the Southland our people were building churches, building schools, having conventions, menfolks trying to vote. From the *Tribune* I also learned of a colored woman in Connecticut who had been a slave in Georgia. That woman left in her will $750 to be used for religious instruction of colored people in Georgia."

"You seem sad."

"I miss the *Tribune*."

"Where it went to?"

"Mr. Deveaux had to shut it down because white print-ers made a pact, said they would no longer take work from a colored man."

Essie decided to spare Binah the tragedies the *Tribune* carried. Accounts of outrages against colored folks by white men, like the two who shot an old man named John near Cochran—and right in front of his wife—because he wasn't moving fast enough in getting their cart unstuck in a rut.

When articles in the *Tribune* made her stomach hurt, Essie read advertisements instead.

James Jefferson's Barber Saloon on the corner of State and Whitaker ... JP Kendy's grocery store ... Eugene Morehead's Forest City Bar and Restaurant ... Her favor-ite was for Clapp's 99 Cents Store on Broughton. "See what 99 cents will buy," it began. "Ladies' Trimmed Hats, Hair Braids and Switches, Shawls, Skirts, Kid Gloves, Silk Ties, Hose, Handkerchiefs, Leather Traveling Bags ..." The list went on and on.

And now, thanks to Dorcas Vashon, Essie had a reason to go to Clapp's and buy a leather traveling bag.

A WIDER WORLD

"Promise me, Binah, promise me you will learn to read," Essie urged again as the girls left the attic, Binah with the wall shelf under her long arm, Essie carrying the books and magazines.

Binah, pretty pliant on most things, had repeatedly refused to let Essie teach her to read, to write.

"With half the boarders being teachers you have a golden opportunity," said Essie as the girls made their way to the kitchen.

"Now, Essie, please don't start that again. You make me nervous. I just know that if I learn to read my head will hurt. I don't know how you hold in all what you read. My head fill up more fastly than yourn."

"Don't you want me to write to you?"

Binah nodded.

"Well, how will you——"

"Will get Miss Abby or a boarder to read your letters to me."

"What if they are too busy?"

Binah had her thinking face on. "I'll just look at the words and conjure up what you likely wrote. Besides, nobody be busy forever."

As the girls dusted, swept, mopped, scrubbed, washed walls room by room, dumped on the back porch anything that was cloth or broken or just didn't seem right, Binah peppered Essie with questions about her soon-coming new life.

"What again is the word for what you will be to Miss Dorcas?"

"Companion."

"Companion," Binah whispered. Cocking her head to the side, she asked, "That like company?"

"Yes, indeed. I will be keeping her company. I imagine I'll be doing things like being by her side when she goes for walks . . . reading books and magazines to her in the evenings. Being someone she can talk to."

"You will also help her keep house?"

"No." Essie smiled. "Remember, I told you that I will be learning to be a lady."

"In a few years' time won't you be a lady anyways?"

"Not as in grown woman, Binah. Lady as in someone who knows how to do things proper."

"Like what?"

"Like how to speak—like just now I should have said someone who knows how to do things *properly*."

"Like what else?"

"The correct way to walk, sit, stand."

"What's wrong with the way you do all that now?"

"It's country."

Essie wished she hadn't put it that way. Binah looked wounded. "What I mean is, Dorcas Vashon will introduce me to society." Essie liked saying the woman's first and last names. "Dorcas Vashon" sounded so strong. Fancy too.

Essie's imagination rolled on. "There'll be elegant dress balls . . . picnics in parks . . . luncheons . . . teas . . . banquets . . . concerts. Dorcas Vashon will introduce me to better things, a wider world, a more wonderful world."

Binah shook her head. "Sounds too much for me. I like my world small. No chance I get lost." After a pause, Binah asked, "You ain't afraid of getting lost in this wider world?"

Essie smiled. "No, Binah. Dorcas Vashon said I will live and breathe and have my being among colored people of rank and prosperity."

"What if something happens to Miss Dorcas? She old, could die any day. Then you'll be away from here all alonely."

That wiped the smile off Essie's face. She had never thought of anything happening to Dorcas Vashon.

She scrubbed the kitchen floor harder, pushing back against a sudden wave of worry.

DONE!

Finish up with Lawyer Logan. *Done!*

Teach the new girl the boardinghouse rules. *Done!*

Buy a leather traveling bag from Clapp's. *Done!*

Pack. *Done!*

The day before she and Dorcas Vashon were to board the *Saragossa*, Essie paid a final visit to Shad Island.

"What is this?" asked Ma Clara when Essie handed her the envelope.

They were sitting in the rockers on Ma Clara's small spring-green back porch.

"Deed to the house on Minis Street," said Essie, bursting with pride. "Lawyer Logan worked it all out."

"Deed?"

"House is yours now, Ma Clara. It passed to me. I pass

it to you. You can sell it. You can make it a boardinghouse. You can . . ."

Ma Clara's mouth fell open.

Essie chuckled. It was the first time she'd seen the woman flummoxed.

Then Ma Clara frowned. "Back up a minute." She raised an eyebrow. "Did you say Lawyer Logan had a hand in this?"

"Yessum. Seeing as how I had to get things tied up fast I figured what with his father being a judge and what with him having a cousin who's a clerk in the courthouse—"

"What did he charge you?"

"Nothing. I only had to pay a small, what they call a filing fee."

"Well, I'll be . . . Never knew that man had a heart."

"Ma Clara, of all Mamma's gentlemen friends Lawyer Logan was one of two who never tried to pat some part of me. But just in case, I took Binah with me both times I went to his office."

Ma Clara held the document at arm's length, squinted, then proceeded to read it out loud. "This Indenture made this 18th day of July 1881 by & between Essie Mirth the party of the first part and Clara Wiggins the party of the second part witnesseth: That the said first party, in consideration of the matters herein of the mentioned, hath this day bargained and sold, conveyed & confirmed unto the said second party, her heirs & assigns, foreon, that certain lot or parcel of land situate, lying & being in the City of Savannah . . ."

"Whatever you decide to do with it, I figure you won't have to clean houses no more, or at least not as many." Choked up, Essie paused, took a deep breath. "Should more than make up for you losing work at Mamma's because of me."

Ma Clara looked at Essie for a long minute. "Let me tell you something."

Essie saw that Ma Clara was getting choked up too.

"If it wasn't for you, I never would have worked for your ma. Not in a million years."

Essie was stunned. "If it wasn't for *me*?"

"Many a day folks asked me how I could work in a house like that." Ma Clara wiped her eyes. " 'For the child's sake,' I told them. 'For the child's sake . . . That house on Minis Street is my mission field,' I explained."

Essie let the tears flow. "Oh, Ma Clara!" She threw herself at the old woman's feet, hugged her with all her might. "Bless your heart, bless your heart, Ma Clara, for all you've done for me. Wasn't for you I—the house, it don't begin to repay you."

"Up, Essie, up." Ma Clara rose too, held Essie by the shoulders. "Essie, look at me and hear me good." When the two were eye to eye Ma Clara continued. "True, I've been a help to you over the years, but *you* saved yourself. *You!*"

"But—"

"You about to argue with me?"

Essie laughed.

Ma Clara laughed.

Both sat back down in the rockers.

To stem the tide of tears, young woman, old woman gazed at the herb garden, Ma Clara's pride. Stands of pennyroyal, yellow dock, bright-yellow tansies, bright-green thyme, white yarrow, rosemary, lovage, and lavender. In the center of the small backyard ringed with cabbage palms, Ma Clara also had a patch of tangerine butterfly weed.

"If you want to repay me," Ma Clara finally said. "You make the most—*the very most*—of this here chance Dorcas Vashon is giving you."

"I promise, Ma Clara, I promise. And I promise to write to you every week."

Ma Clara pshawed. "Girlene, you will be so busy you won't have time to be writing me."

Essie saw something odd in Ma Clara's eyes.

"You promise me now that you will give first focus to your lady lessons. Let all of that be the apple of your eye."

What was it? Ma Clara was hiding something.

After a few squeaks from her rocker, Ma Clara added, "Essie, I don't need letters. Wherever you are, I will be with you in spirit."

Tears were on the rise again as it dawned on Essie that had it not been for Ma Clara she never would have crossed paths with Dorcas Vashon.

She owed Ma Clara everything.

ALWAYS YOU'LL BE HERE

"Your favorite off-work dress!"

Essie relished Binah's joy gushing up as she stroked the light-pink gingham dress.

"This is really mine now? To keep?"

"Yes, indeed," said Essie. "Along with my other two," she added, pointing to her sky-blue and pale yellow calicos. "And here." Essie reached under her bed and brought out a pair of shoes. "These, too," she added with a nod at the lace bonnet and the straw bonnet hanging on nails above her bed.

"Who would have thought I'd *ever* have *five* dresses and *two* pair of nice shoes. Four hats too!"

"And some good news, Binah," Essie said with a lilt in her voice. "Clara Wiggins said she would be pleased as punch for you to call her Ma Clara. She will look in on you from time to time. And you are welcome to visit her on your day off."

"Oh, thank you, Essie!"

The two girls hugged.

"I will miss you so very much, Binah," said Essie, trying not to cry.

Not Binah. She was in tears. "I will miss you a mighty amount," she said. "But you won't be truly gone, Essie," Binah added between sniffles. She placed her right hand over her heart. "Always you'll be here."

QUEEN OF SEA ROUTES

After tearful goodbyes with Miss Abby, with Binah, on the morning of Tuesday, July 19, 1881, Essie helped Dorcas Vashon into a jet-black carriage. The driver had already loaded their luggage.

As the horses clip-clopped, clip-clopped down one street, then another . . .

Past shops . . .

Past stalls . . .

Past Geechee women strolling strong with baskets atop their heads, some filled with vegetables, others with she-crabs wriggling in nets.

Past warehouses with bales of cotton, tierces of rice . . .

Past the redbrick buildings that made up Factors Row . . .

Essie pinched herself.

Once she and Dorcas Vashon were settled on board the *Saragossa*, Essie took a turn on the deck by herself.

The night before she had decided against traveling in her fancy black dress. Instead she wore the silk heliotrope with sleeves and hem finished in an eggshell lace and with a cape of nun's veiling. Her white straw bonnet was trimmed with satin and feathers.

"Heliotrope," Dorcas Vashon had explained, "is a symbol of eternal love. Also fortitude."

Essie felt that fortitude as she watched the waves, took in the smoke billowing from chimneys, church spires piercing the sky. "Farewell, Forest City," she whispered, remembering that three-masted ship painted on the inside of the lid of her long-gone battered sea chest.

As the *Saragossa* moved farther out to sea, Essie recalled reading that the firm that owned the *Saragossa* and many other steamships prided itself as the "Queen of Sea Routes."

A princess. That's what she felt like in her heliotrope dress. Her new black lace-up boots still pinched, but she knew it would only be a matter of time before her feet would be fine. Also new was her purse: yellow silk overlaid with lace. Inside was a handkerchief, the pocket watch Dorcas Vashon had gifted her with, and those twenty-five coral beads.

With Factors Row and the rest of the Savannah harbor looking smaller and smaller, with her past growing misty, Essie felt foolish for holding on to those beads. She opened her purse ready to toss them, one by one, into the sea.

Something stopped her.

Another thought took its place.

For a new life she desired a new name, a name befitting a lady.

Later that night she told Dorcas Vashon of her decision to change her name.

Dorcas Vashon looked up from her tea. "What is it, my dear?"

Essie felt sheepish. Something about saying it out loud frightened her. Then she cleared her throat, held her head high.

"Well, my dear, what is your new name?"

"Victoria."

Said with all the fortitude that she could muster.

FIRST-FLOOR SHUTTERS
ASKEW

As she walked down the gangplank of the *Saragossa*, as
the driver loaded their luggage, helped Dorcas Vashon,
then her into his coach, Victoria did her best to hold her
breath.

Baltimore's harbor stank worse than Savannah's. Or was
it just a different kind of stink? The place seemed noisier,
too, with a greater babble of tongues.

"*A broch!*" shouted a man in all black, when the rope
around his suitcase broke and his belongings tumbled out.
Victoria wondered where he was from.

A spindly woman with two small children straggling
behind her, a woman with bundles in her hands, bundles
under her arms—

"*Kommen, Kinder!*" she yelled.

Furiously waving his hands to get someone's attention,
a short, olive-skinned young man cried out, "*Thar anseo!
Thar anseo!*"

And stevedores were cussing up a storm.

A stately home, brick or stone. Long driveway. A sumptuous garden. Perhaps even a fountain out front—that's the kind of home Victoria imagined they were bound for.

When rich people returned from a journey, their servants lined up outside to greet them, Victoria had read. While she and Binah had worn everyday clothes at Miss Abby's, Victoria was certain that Dorcas Vashon's maids would be in proper pressed black dresses with lace cuffs and collars. The butler too.

Not in a black dress but in a proper butler's—

Livery. That's what it was called. Bright-white shirt. Cutaway coat. Striped trousers. Vest. White gloves.

A housekeeper would also be waiting for them. Footmen. Coach—

Alarm bells went off in Victoria's head.

Surely, a woman of Dorcas Vashon's wealth had a fine black carriage and a coachman to drive it. So why were they in this rickety mud-brown coach? The driver was a grizzly old man in seedy gray homespun pants and dingy white collarless shirt. He had a frayed straw hat cocked on his head.

Joy waned, fear rose as the two dirty white horses clip-clopped on.

Down one narrow street after another.

Tiny houses jammed together one after the other after the . . .

Stretches of plain brick houses, many a sallow red.

Some had no steps leading up to front doors. Others three cold-white steps. Railings were nonexistent or skimpy. Nothing fanciful and festive like the ironwork in Forest City.

"Why Savannah called Forest City?" she had asked Ma Clara when very young.

"Think about it, Essie. How far can you go without seeing a live oak, magnolia, palm, or a multitude of other trees? Especially a live oak."

She had then asked Ma Clara why a certain oak was called "live" and Ma Clara spoke of legends surrounding Spanish moss.

Of the Spanish soldier lashed to a tree for his love affair with the daughter of a Cherokee chieftain. "That soldier could only be set free," cooed Ma Clara, "if he vowed to stop loving that Indian girl. Again and again he refused. All the while his beard grew and grew and grew even after he perished, parched and starved."

Would someone ever love her that much, little Essie had wondered.

"Some say Spanish moss come from the long hair of a princess slain by a Spanish soldier," Ma Clara continued. "Hair was slung up high in a tree and somehow it spread from one oak to another to another."

*   *   *

Clip-clop, clip-clop.

A rattled Victoria pined to be Essie again and back in Forest City.

Baltimore was scary. Something was terribly wrong.

Fortitude! she urged herself as here and there she spied droopy flowers—geraniums, poppies, daisies, begonias—in window boxes, but not a single flower garden out front.

On most of the narrow streets not even a tree.

Fortitude!

Victoria felt a stomachache coming on when the coach stopped before a lonesome three-story brick house on a street behind God's back.

What is this? Is Dorcas Vashon dropping something off to someone? Looking in on someone? But Victoria couldn't fathom Dorcas Vashon associating with anyone who lived in a house like this, in this cheerless alley.

No railing for the three steps that led to its weather-beaten pale-blue front door. Wooden shutters the only touch of adornment. Weather-beaten. Pale blue, too, with first-floor shutters askew.

Is this my wider world?

BALLERINA LEGS

The luggage was in the house and that grizzly driver long gone.

"Victoria, what has come over you?" Dorcas Vashon stood inside the small front hall, beckoning her inside. "Come along, now."

What else could Victoria do? She didn't know a soul in Baltimore. Home was a three-day sea ride, hundreds of miles away.

Victoria entered the house.

It smelled clean.

Hints of cedarwood and lemon.

Floors of herringbone pine polished to a high shine.

That narrow house with first-floor shutters askew was eerily quiet.

"Parlor," Dorcas Vashon said softly of the room to the left of the entranceway, a room that took Victoria's breath away.

It was finer than Miss Abby's parlor. A marble-topped table. At the window creamy gold heavy draperies with more material across the top. A few feet in front of the window a five-legged settee in a soft coral color, coral like azaleas, coral like those beads. Victoria guessed the upholstery to be silk, as she marveled that the settee's honey-brown wood had such elaborate carving. Fruit, flowers, leaves. On its wings there were more intricately carved flowers but in urns. The settee's five legs—three in the front, two in the back—brought to mind a picture Victoria had seen, perhaps in *Oliver Optic's Magazine*, of a ballerina up on her toes. But the settee as a whole made Victoria think not of a dancer but of a winged creature—like a vulture—poised to take flight.

The table before the settee also had ballerina legs.

There was nothing on the walls except a large round mirror over the fireplace. Was the frame real gold? The crystals in the chandelier shined like diamonds. A triangular bookcase in one corner of the room filled Victoria with a measure of comfort.

The small dining room behind the parlor was even more of a wonderland with clusters of grapes and tender leaves adorning the pierced-back chairs with plump royal-blue seats. Matching buffet, sideboard, table—a table that puzzled Victoria. It was too large for the room. There was barely enough room to walk on either side of this table that sat eight.

Who else lives here?

"Take up your bags, now, and follow me," said Dorcas Vashon.

On the second-floor landing Dorcas Vashon pointed to the front room on the right. "My bedroom." Down the hall to the left—

"Your bedroom."

When Dorcas Vashon opened that door Victoria lit up. The narrow bed that ended where the window began was something for a princess. High arched footboard. The headboard was higher still with a more pronounced arch. Atop it was something like a crown of carved flowers. Bedstead to wardrobe to washstand, all the furniture was burl, just like the furniture in Miss Abby's Room #4.

The ivory curtains were meanders of leaves, flowers, branches. Soft greens, rose, pale gold. Here and there a chipper squirrel perched on a branch.

A much-relieved Victoria was on the point of gushing. "What a lovely room," she whispered.

"Tea at two," said Dorcas Vashon as she left the room, closing the door behind her.

Victoria reached into her purse for her pocket watch.

Hurriedly she washed her face, changed out of her traveling clothes, and donned her daffodil day dress. Before she left her bedroom she checked her hair in the mirror above the washstand. When she headed down for tea Victoria was measurably less uneasy than when she first laid eyes on that alley house with first-floor shutters askew.

That ease, however, was short-lived.

GAUCHE

Bleak.

Such were Victoria's first days in Baltimore, days of bashful sun and a cloying dampness.

Nothing for her to do but read newspapers, books. Dorcas Vashon cautioned her against—more like forbade her from—going outside, other than out back: an eight-by-eight bit of concrete. Walled in. Victoria reckoned the wooden planks, fifteen, twenty feet high.

No real conversation during meals. Only commands.

"Sit up straight, my dear."

"Do not slurp your soup, my dear."

"Small bites, my dear."

"Always leave a bit on your plate, my dear. A clean plate is gauche."

Gauche? Victoria had never heard that word before but figured it kin to "wrong" or "country."

Wide stride walking, holding a fork in a grip, running upstairs—Victoria learned that so much of what she did was—

"That is gauche, my dear."

My dear. My dear. My dear.

But Dorcas Vashon never made Victoria feel one bit dear. Only *gauche*.

Victoria was beginning to fear those eyes again.

There were smiles with each "my dear," but Dorcas Vashon's tone was cold. Come to think of it, after they left Savannah the woman had less and less to say to her. She recalled, too, that during the voyage she had told her that in Baltimore the first lesson would be on patience.

Victoria felt trapped. The silence was suffocating, maddening.

"Would you like me to read to you, Miss Dorcas?"

"Would you . . . ?"

Responses were usually a one-word "No." Or "No thank you, my dear."

Miss Doone, the light-skinned gnomelike cleaner, never said a mumbling word to Victoria. The most she ever heard her say to Dorcas Vashon was, "Yes, ma'am," or "Will do, ma'am," or "Surely."

Miss Graves, a pinch-faced, spindly, dark-skinned woman, lived where she worked. Down in the basement where the kitchen was placed. Dorcas Vashon had yet to show Victoria the kitchen. On the day they arrived in Baltimore, she had only pointed to the door that led down to it and said, "The kitchen is down there."

Just then Victoria processed something she hadn't realized she'd seen when she first laid eyes on that narrow house with first-floor shutters askew. Out front, there were two small windows near the ground. Later, when she met Miss Graves, Victoria imagined the kitchen faced the small windows and that behind it was Miss Graves's room.

Victoria only saw Miss Graves when the woman brought meals up to the dining room. She never cleared the table until Dorcas Vashon and Victoria had left the room.

"This is where I'm to live . . . forever?" Victoria summoned up the courage to ask over breakfast one day.

Dorcas Vashon shook her head. "Just for a time, until you are ready."

"How will I get ready?"

"Miss Hardwick. She will arrive soon. She will train you."

"In what?"

"Everything."

*   *   *

In the meantime Dorcas Vashon began teaching Victoria about important colored people. Her textbook was mostly the *People's Advocate*. "It is published in Washington, DC," Dorcas Vashon explained. "You must read this newspaper diligently as I have been doing in adding to my knowledge about colored society in the capital. There are some people I especially want you to be on the lookout for in the pages of the *Advocate*, people you may very well meet." Then came the start of a list.

John Wesley Cromwell, the editor of the *Advocate*: "He rose up from slavery to attend Howard University's law school. Along with managing the *Advocate*, he holds a prized job at a post office in the national capital."

Daniel Alexander Payne Murray: "He is the assistant librarian of the congressional library. He has done very well for himself thanks to shrewd investments in real estate."

John Mercer Langston: "He is a graduate of Oberlin College and Ohio's first colored lawyer. Back after the war, about a year after Howard University was founded, he launched its law school. He is now an ambassador, to Haiti.

"You have heard of Howard University?"

"Yessum."

Dorcas Vashon made a face. "Remember, Victoria, as I told you on the ship and as I have told you several times since we reached Baltimore, 'Yessum' is—"

"Gauche. Yes, ma'am. I'm sorr—my apologies, ma'am." Victoria felt like such an oaf.

And there was James Wormley: "He owns one of the finest hotels in the nation's capital. It is a favorite of big, important white men in business and in government. Some even live there. Wormley's is also very popular with European visitors. When President Garfield was shot, Wormley was called upon to make special broths."

O. S. B. Wall: "Another graduate of Oberlin, another lawyer. First colored justice of the peace in Washington, he was a police magistrate too. John Mercer Langston married his sister, Caroline, who also attended Oberlin. What a fine pair they must make!" O. S. B. Wall's full name, Victoria next heard, was Orindatus Simon Bolívar Wall.

"Are you paying attention, my dear?"

Victoria's mind had wandered. "I'm sorry, ma'am. It's just that . . ."

"What?"

"It's a lot to take in."

"It is indeed. That is why if at some point you do not understand something you should ask a question. Never pretend that you know something, understand something when you do not. Now, do you have any questions?"

"What, where is Oberin?"

"O-ber-*lin*. It is a college in Oberlin, Ohio, one of the first colleges to admit our people. That was in the 1830s."

Victoria couldn't imagine colored folks going to college way back then!

"Anything else?"

"The man with all those names? Opin . . ."

"Orindatus. 'Orin' is a Celtic name, and 'datus' is Latin for 'given.'" After a pause Dorcas Vashon added, " 'Celtic' means pertaining to the Celts, an ancient people."

"I was just about to ask," said Victoria, then took a sip of tea.

"And of course in the capital we have the honorable Frederick Douglass," said Dorcas Vashon one day. "He lives across the Anacostia River on his estate, Cedar Hill. His mansion has more than twenty rooms. You do know who Frederick Douglass is?"

"Yes, ma'am, I do," Victoria said with pride. "Read his book at Miss Abby's."

"Which one?"

Victoria felt dumb again. She lowered her head. "I only know of one."

Dumb and scatterbrained. Now she couldn't remember the book's title.

Finally it came to her. "*My Bondage and My Freedom*, that's the one I read." She swallowed. "It was awful powerful," she added, trying to sound intelligent.

"That would be his second autobiography," replied Dorcas Vashon. "I believe a third is on the way. As well, my dear, the honorable Frederick Douglass wrote a novella."

Teatime again, with Victoria charged with pouring when the clock on the mantelpiece struck two.

What a strange clock it was. A brown wooden item in the shape of a church, its base a scary tangle of gnarled roots. Every half hour the church door opened and out came a monk with a long white beard ringing a bell. Spooky-looking clock, like something you'd find in an ugly hut in a dark, dense forest, the kind of thing the witch who kidnapped Hansel and Gretel would have. Though Victoria couldn't imagine a witch having much use for a monk.

"When reading, if you encounter a word that you do not know," said Dorcas Vashon over supper one day, "never be content to remain ignorant. If you cannot figure it out, take up your dictionary."

Dorcas Vashon told her on another day about the Greens . . . the Syphaxes . . . the Cooks . . . the Bruces . . . Dr. Charles Purvis . . . Milton Holland. Dorcas Vashon steadily fed Victoria more names.

Patience.

Victoria was getting the hang of being patient at meals. Getting used to being patient as she waited for her new life to begin, but that patience grew thin when Dorcas Vashon delivered a devastating blow.

DORCAS VASHON IS A MONSTER!

With all the energy spent adjusting to that house with first-floor shutters askew, Victoria had plum forgot about writing home until one day she was up in her room reading the *Advocate*, grateful for the sunshine and the chirp of birds. The squirrels on her curtain even seemed more chipper.

"I got seasick a couple times, but all in all I held up pretty well. I made a big decision. I changed my name to Victoria. So from now on I am Victoria Mirth. How do you like my new name? Please write soon." So ended her letter to Ma Clara.

Victoria was about to start one to Binah when it hit her. No envelopes. Why would a desk have an ample supply of notepaper, pen and ink, but no envelopes? She searched every cubby, every drawer of the rolltop desk.

A sinking feeling set in as she realized something else. Victoria closed her eyes, racked her brains. She sent herself back to the day they pulled up to the house.

Was there a number on the front door?

A street sign?

Victoria grew increasingly anxious.

She didn't know where she was. No reference. No compass point.

She went to Dorcas Vashon's closed bedroom door. She knocked.

No answer.

She headed downstairs and found her in the parlor reading the *Evening Star.*

"Miss Dorcas?" Victoria asked timidly.

"Yes, my dear?"

"What is the address here?"

Dorcas Vashon grimaced. "What is the address here? Why would you need that information?"

"I'm writing to Ma Clara, Binah, and Miss Abby. Also I need envelopes."

Dorcas looked even more cross. "My dear Victoria. I thought you understood. You must cut all ties."

Victoria frowned. "What do you mean?"

"You are here to prepare for your future. There's to be no looking back."

"But I just want to write to them."

"Eyes forward, Victoria. Eyes forward."

Stunned and spitting mad, Victoria hung her head, tried to control herself. *Dorcas Vashon is a monster!*

"Remember, my dear, in Savannah I told you to sleep on my offer, to decide if you could leave the life you had behind and cut all ties."

"I didn't understand you meant—"

"I have already sent word to Abby and Clara that you are safe and sound. Before we left, I told Clara not to expect to hear from you directly."

Girlene, you will be so busy you won't have time to be writing me.

No wonder Ma Clara's odd look. She knew.

Victoria stomped her foot. "Miss Dorcas, this ain't fair. Why didn't you tell me I wouldn't be able to even *write* to them?"

Dorcas Vashon is a monster!

The eyes were knives. "What do you think cutting all ties means? You are brighter than that. And you were bold enough to discard the name your mother gave you." Dorcas Vashon rose, began to pace. "And tell me this, Victoria. Had I told you specifically that you would not be able to write to people back home would you have declined my offer?"

The question wounded more than the look.

Victoria trudged back up to her room, wrestling with a new shame.

Had I told you specifically that you would not be able to write to people back home would you have declined my offer?

There had been no quick, decisive *NO!*

Am I a monster too?

NIBBLING

Patience.

With the silence.

With the loneliness.

With doubts.

With tea sandwiches at teatime, repressing the urge to gulp one down with a single bite. Nibbling instead as instructed.

Rectangular ones of creamed butter and egg salad.

Round ones of cucumber and dill with a pale-yellow spread on the soft bread.

Triangle-shaped ones of potted salmon and a plant similar to what she'd grown up calling creasy greens.

As she nibbled, read books, read newspapers, learned the word "watercress," Victoria no longer wondered where her wider world would be.

Washington, DC, the national capital!

Not Baltimore. Everyone Dorcas Vashon talked about, told her to learn about, was in Washington, DC. Not Baltimore.

Your journey would begin in Baltimore. That's what Dorcas Vashon had said back in Forest City.

Begin.

Not end!

Hope bestirred again, Victoria read the newspapers more intently.

Everything. Miss Hardwick would teach her everything.

Victoria couldn't wait for her arrival. She vowed to be the very best pupil, to work hard. The harder she worked, the sooner she'd be delivered from the queer house with first-floor shutters askew.

A CREATURE TO BE FEARED

The woman arrived on a dreary, sun-starved day.

Hawk nose. Amber antelope eyes. Caramel skin. Big-boned, giant Agnes Hardwick made Victoria think of a griffin she had seen—she couldn't remember where. In *Oliver Optic's*? A book at Miss Abby's? But Victoria did remember this: a griffin, half eagle, half lion, was a creature to be feared.

The way Miss Hardwick looked her over brought to mind taunts of Sarah Pace.

Essie is messy!

Gutter girl!

Your ma is a—!

The woman sniffed as if downwind of a pigsty.

Stiff as a board, Victoria stood in the archway between entrance hall and parlor staring down at the herringbone pine floor.

Miss Hardwick hmmed, huffed, sighed.

Victoria felt like a horse or a cow for sale as she looked out of the corner of her eye at a big black leather bag and a bigger brown suitcase.

Finally Miss Hardwick spoke: "Follow me, please." She took her luggage in hand, headed for the stairs.

Victoria followed, up to the second floor, up to the third, where she had never been before. A time or two, on her way to bed, she had been tempted to tiptoe up to the third floor, but she always lost her nerve.

Some days while in the parlor reading the *Advocate* or the *Evening Star* she had watched Miss Doone head up the stairs with bucket and brushes and rags. The footsteps told her when the woman was going to clean her room or Dorcas Vashon's and when Miss Doone was going to the third floor. Not every time she came. Occasionally Victoria heard Dorcas Vashon go up to the third floor, enter the room above Victoria's bedroom, then begin to pace.

Someone living up there?

A madwoman like in Jane Eyre*?*

An invalid, maybe?

Someone horribly scarred? In such a bad way he—or she—needed to be kept out of sight?

Surely Victoria would have heard noises other than her benefactor's pacing. A cough, a moan. Something.

Maybe the poor invalid can't speak, can't hear.

But she never saw Miss Graves go upstairs with a tray of food.

When they reached the third-floor landing—

"Wait here."

Miss Hardwick set her black bag down, then headed for the front room with her suitcase. Victoria craned her neck hoping for a peek into the room. Before Miss Hardwick shut the door, all Victoria glimpsed was a bed with a burl bedstead and off-white coverlet.

Miss Hardwick wasn't gone long. When she returned, Victoria faced front. Miss Hardwick picked up her black bag and headed down the hall to the back room.

With her hand on the doorknob Miss Hardwick said nothing, only beckoned.

Victoria obeyed not knowing what in the world to expect.

E-TI-KET

A schoolroom.

Wide chalkboard along one wall. Before it an oak desk and ladder-back chair. The desk was bigger than Miss Purdy's. Next to the desk a lectern. In the middle of the room a lone pupil's desk.

Another wall was a floor-to-ceiling bookcase with not a space to spare. Victoria found all those books overwhelming. Like Miss Hardwick, they made her feel so small.

Victoria shifted from foot to foot, watching Miss Hardwick bring out things from her black bag and place them on her desk: clock, small pointer, chalk, little brass bell, brown ink bottle, brown inkwell, dip pen.

"Have a seat, please."

Victoria obeyed.

Miss Hardwick began to pace before her. "You went how far in school?"

"Only for about a year."

"What grade?"

"First."

"My goodness. I had no idea it would be this bad."

"But after I—"

"Why did you leave school?"

Victoria hesitated. "Other kids, they teased me."

"About what?"

Victoria shaved the truth. "About being poor."

"So you did not value education?"

"No, Miss Hardwick, I did, I—"

"Victoria, if you had *valued* education, you would *not* have left school. You *would* have *persevered*."

Victoria lowered her head. "But I did—"

"Look up, young lady. Always look up when in conversation. Always look up when walking. Always look up even while eating. Never hang your head. Now, you were saying?"

So nervous, Victoria couldn't remember. She wrung her hands, bit her lip. Then it came to her.

"With all due respect, Miss Hardwick, I did value education, so much so that after I left school I bought books and magazines from a secondhand store. I—I read whenever I could, and Ma Clara—well, this woman who was kind to me—used to give me newspapers after she finished with them. I read every one she passed down to me, colored paper it was." Victoria swallowed. "After that paper went away I bought with my own money Savannah's white paper."

Victoria thought she saw a hint of a smile when Miss Hardwick responded, "Perhaps there is hope for you yet."

Miss Hardwick returned to her big desk and to her black bag. Out came two books. She placed one on her desk, handed the other to Victoria.

"We will start with this. Let it be your Bible. Title page, please. Read it."

Victoria turned to the page. Her heart sank.

"The—The Ladies' Book of—"

"*E*-ti-ket."

"*E*-ti-ket." Victoria repeated hitting the *t* and the *k* as hard as Miss Hardwick had.

"Do you know the meaning of 'etiquette'?"

"No, ma'am."

"Your answer is insufficient."

"But, ma'am, I truly don't—"

"You should have replied along the lines of this: 'No, Miss Hardwick, I do not know the meaning of the word "etiquette."'"

Victoria lowered her head, but only for an instant. Looking up at Miss Hardwick she said, "No, Miss Hardwick, I do not know the meaning of the word 'etiquette.'"

Again a hint of a smile.

"Etiquette is polite behavior, decorum, good form."

She lost Victoria after "polite behavior."

"Continue reading."

"and Manual of—"

"From the beginning."

Victoria cleared her throat. "The Ladies' Book of Etiquette, and Manual of Politeness."

"Continue."

"A Complete Hand Book for the Use of the Lady in Polite Society."

"Continue."

"Containing Full Directions for Correct Manners, Dress, De— Depot—"

"Deportment." Miss Hardwick was pacing again.

"Deportment."

"Do you know the meaning of the word 'deportment'?"

"No, ma—I mean, no, Miss Hardwick, I do not know the meaning of the word 'deportment.'"

"Deportment is how one carries oneself—in private and in public. Does one move, sit, stand, like a queen or a country bumpkin?"

Victoria nodded rapidly, keeping her head up.

"Continue," commanded the Griffin.

"Deportment and Conversation; Rules for the Duties of Both Hostess and Guest in Morning Receptions, Dinner Companies—"

"Sit up straight. Hold the book twelve to fourteen inches from your face and keep your head up."

Victoria made the adjustments, wondering if "morning receptions" was a fancy way of saying "breakfast."

"Continue."

"Dinner Companies, Visiting, Evening Parties and Balls; A Complete Guide for Letter Writing and Cards of Compliment; Hints on Managing Servants, on the Preservation of Health, and on Accomplishments."

"Is something wrong?"

"No, Miss Hardwick." Victoria took a deep breath, continued reading. "And Also Useful Receipts for the Complexion, Hair, And with Hints for the Care of the Wardrobe. By Florence Hartley."

Wardrobe as in a piece of furniture or clothes?

At the bottom of the page Victoria saw that this was not Miss Florence Hartley's only book. She had also written the *Ladies Hand Book of Fancy and Ornamental Work.*

Victoria's heart was in her mouth. *Will I have to read that book too?*

"Now turn to Contents."

Victoria tried to steady her hands as she turned pages. She gulped when she reached Contents. "You want me to read all this too?"

"Victoria, your question is wrongly put. What you should have asked is this: 'Miss Hardwick, do you wish for me to read all of this as well?' In polite society it is bad form to be stingy with words."

Victoria took another deep breath. "Miss Hardwick, do you wish for me to read all of this as well?"

"There is no need for that, Victoria. However, I would like you to review the contents."

Victoria caught herself slouching. She straightened her back, steadied her hand as she stared at the Contents page.

"Conversation" was followed by "Dress" was followed by "Traveling." On and on it went.

"How to Behave at a Hotel" . . . "Visiting—Etiquette for the Hostess" . . . "Visiting—Etiquette for the Guest" . . . "Table Etiquette" . . . "Conduct in the Street" . . . "Letter Writing" . . . "On a Young Lady's Conduct when Contemplating Marriage . . ."

The book was over three hundred pages long. Victoria had a monstrous headache. It wasn't that she had never read books that long, but they were novels, biographies, autobiographies, not books crammed with rules.

"Let it be your Bible," Miss Hardwick said again. She then proceeded to inform Victoria of her schedule.

Before Miss Hardwick dismissed Victoria she made her hold out her hands.

Palms up.

Palms down.

"You have been in service."

Victoria nodded.

"The feet, please?"

Victoria took off her stockings, her shoes.

Heel up.

Heel down.

Heel up.

Heel down.

Victoria was awash with shame as Miss Hardwick inspected her feet.

"I see that you have been allowed to go about barefoot," said the Griffin with raised eyebrows. Victoria felt like a mangy cur dog.

When dismissed, Victoria couldn't get her stockings and shoes on quickly enough, couldn't get to her room fast enough. Once inside, back pressed against the closed door she burst into tears, clamped a hand over her mouth.

Get ahold of yourself!

She couldn't.

Victoria wrapped her arms around herself when the tears subsided. Limply, listlessly she walked over to the narrow window.

Dorcas Vashon had instructed her to keep the curtains drawn always. And she did, but occasionally she peeked out, as she did now.

A tubby man in a brown sack coat and brown pants and wearing a broad-brimmed hat walked briskly past a lanky lad leading a pony cart loaded with melons.

Farther down the street, a woman in a dingy check gingham dress was scolding a little girl.

Next door, a wide, squat woman was scrubbing three front steps.

Laughter rose from the street below. Hearty laughter.

From afar steamboat whistles and honks, horses in a trot.

Victoria wondered about the people she saw on the street. Was the tubby man a butcher? Baker? Had the lad's family grown those melons? What had the little girl done to make the woman in the dingy check gingham so cross? Was the wide, squat woman the Missus of the house or a servant? Whoever they were, Victoria envied them. They were out and about, living.

They didn't appear to have a worry in the world about their deportment and *e-ti-ket*.

FILLING UP TOO FASTLY

The hushed house had more routine than Miss Abby's.

Rise at six o'clock, followed by breakfast at seven o'clock, followed by lessons—etiquette, elocution, deportment—followed by tea at two, followed by fifteen minutes of walking at a moderate pace in the backyard, followed by more lessons—penmanship and poetry recitation—followed by calisthenics in the backyard, followed by forty-five minutes in her bedroom in quiet contemplation, followed by lessons on the waltz, the two-step, followed by . . .

Daily, along with newspapers, Victoria had to read an assigned passage from *Ladies' Book of Etiquette*. And there was Mrs. Beeton's *Book of Household Management; Comprising Information for the Mistress, Housekeeper, Cook, Kitchen-Maid, Butler, Footman, Coachman, Valet, Upper and Under House-Maids, Lady's-Maid, Maid-of-All-Work,*

Laundry-Maid, Nurse and Nurse-Maid, Monthly, Wet, and Sick Nurses, Etc. Etc. Also . . .

Aloud in the schoolroom, Victoria had to read sections of another Beeton book: *Beeton's Housewife's Treasury of Domestic Information: Comprising Complete and Practical Instructions on the House and Its Furniture, Artistic Decoration, Economy, Toilet, Children—*

There was that word again!

Etiquette.

Followed by *Domestic and Fancy Needlework, Dressmaking and Millinery, and All Other Household Matters: With Every Requisite Direction to Secure the Comfort, Elegance, and Prosperity of the Home.*

The fact that the book was "profusely illustrated" did nothing for Victoria's spirits. When she first scanned the list of illustrations she might as well have been reading a foreign language for the most part.

"Air Brick."

"Bed of Ware, The Great."

"Cantilevers Supporting a Balcony."

"Charlton House, Kent."

This second book of Mrs. Beeton was more than a thousand pages.

Thank heavens the *Spencerian Key to Practical Penmanship* was under two hundred pages. "Position gives power," it stated. "Good penmanship requires an easy, convenient, and healthful position."

Every weekend Victoria had to read a book from the schoolroom's frightening shelves.

Anna Karenina . . . Middlemarch . . . Twenty Thousand Leagues Under the Sea . . . Black Beauty . . . The Mystery of Edwin Drood . . . The Way We Live Now . . .

Inexplicably petrified as she stared at the bookshelf on Miss Hardwick's first Friday, Victoria couldn't pick a book. So much choice was mind-boggling.

"She who hesitates is lost!" snapped Miss Hardwick, standing behind Victoria. The Griffin plucked a book from the shelves and thrust it into Victoria's hands.

Bleak House by Charles Dickens.

Victoria's mouth fell open. That book was so thick, heavy. More than eight hundred pages long.

Lessons on math, history, geography. Needlework. Cooking lessons too. Victoria was most on edge when made to set the dining table.

Knife. Spoon. Fork. That's all she had known at that house on Minis Street. At Miss Abby's too, except there she had learned about butter knives and parfait spoons. Now she had to deal with a dizzying, daunting list, a new deluge of rules.

To the left of the plate: short fork, the salad fork.

"One inch from the table's edge, if you please, like the plate."

Then the longer fork—the dinner fork.

To the right of the plate: long dinner knife—

"Blade facing the plate, please," instructed Miss Hardwick through gritted teeth.

Then the—

"One inch from the table's edge!" the Griffin huffed.

Teaspoon.

Soup spoon.

Parallel to the table's edge: dessert spoon and dessert fork.

Left of the dinner plate a bread plate with a bread knife upon it.

Upper right of the plate: water glass, wine glass.

Victoria fought back tears when Miss Hardwick said, "This is the setting for a simple dinner."

What other kinds of dinners are there?

"For formal affairs . . ."

"Between the salad fork and the dinner fork—" Victoria paused, determined to get it right. "The fork about the size of a salad fork only with three prongs—"

Even when she got it right she was wrong.

"*Tines,*" Miss Hardwick corrected. "*Tines.*"

"Tines," Victoria repeated, upper lip atremble.

"And the name of this fork?"

"Fish fork."

"The dessert spoon and fork above the plate, slightly to the left, making room for a place card," instructed Miss Hardwick. "And if both coffee and tea are to be served . . ."

More formal meant more glasses too. Added to the water goblet . . .

Some nights Victoria couldn't sleep for the clatter in her head—pastry server, bonbon server, stuffing spoon, fish serving knife, fish serving fork, salad servers, asparagus server, sardine tongs, lobster fork, lobster pick, cheese scoop, sugar shell—

Sterling silver versus silver plate. Bone-handled, pearl-handled, onyx—

And every mistake put her in a panic, left her sick inside.

Forgetting the fish knife.

Mixing up the butter *knife* and the butter *spreader.*

Failing to align the utensils with the plate.

Confusing the lemon fork with the oyster fork.

Putting down the wrong soup spoon—

"*Round-bowled* for cream soup, *oval* for clear," Miss Hardwick corrected one day with a huge sigh of disgust. "Abandon all hope, I say," she added under her breath, then to Victoria, "What soup is on tonight's menu?"

"Consommé Robespierre is on tonight's menu, Miss Hardwick."

"And does Consommé Robespierre contain any cream?"

"No, Miss Hardwick, Consommé Robespierre contains no cream."

"Therefore, Victoria, which is the correct soup spoon for tonight's supper?"

"For tonight's supper the correct soup spoon is the oval soup spoon, Miss Hardwick." Now Victoria knew how Binah felt. She couldn't hold on to all this information, all the details. Her head was filling up too fastly.

Ma Clara had always told Victoria how bright she was, and Victoria had always prided herself on her brains, on being smart.

But smart next to who—?

She meant *whom?*

Binah?

Victoria would give anything to be doing simple things.

Reading Binah a story.

Preparing Ma Clara's foot soak.

She missed Binah's carefree ways, Ma Clara's stories.

Miss Abby was on the strict side but nowhere near as demanding as the Griffin.

Life was so much easier in Forest City.

The Blue Willow dishes Victoria and Dorcas Vashon had been eating from was the nicest china Victoria had ever seen, but after the arrival of the Griffin they dined on dishes that belonged in Buckingham Palace.

Heavy crystal glasses.

One set of dinner plates had pink roses on its border. Another yellow pansies. A third was rimmed in gold.

Most intriguing was one set of breakfast dishes. Bright

white with green dragons and phoenixes. The way they swirled around the edge of the plates, the middle of the teacups, Victoria was betwixt and between as to whether they were engaged in a dance or a chase.

And a green phoenix? Whenever Victoria came across any mention of a phoenix it was red. For a phoenix was a fire bird, rising from ashes. Reborn. New. Stronger.

PÄ-ˌTĀ-DƏ-ˌFWÄ-ˈGRÄ

More bewildering was the food, especially dinners.

Up from the basement now came feasts, a daunting array of dishes, many of which gave Victoria a mumble mouth when she first tried to pronounce them.

Like Consommé Robespierre.

Chateaubriand, Potatoes Lyonnaise, Charlotte Russe, Roasted Tongue, Galantine of Game, Venison Chops.

While Victoria's taste buds were getting accustomed to strange new dishes, Dorcas Vashon was usually content with a bowl of soup and a salad, a plate of roasted vegetables, or succotash.

"If you don't mind my asking, Miss Dorcas, why is it that you do not eat meat?" Victoria ventured to ask one day.

"More healthful for me, my dear."

* * *

Ham Timbales.

Timbales à la Rothschild.

Baked Salmon with Sauce Hollandaise.

Broiled Quail.

Roast Canvas-Back Duck.

Terrapin, Stewed à la Willards.

Back home Victoria had only known oysters fried and raw. In Baltimore she learned of Scalloped Oysters, Pickled Oysters, Oysters au Gratin, Oysters à la Poulette.

"Pä-ˌtā-də-ˌfwä-'grä." Miss Hardwick had her say that over and over until she mastered the term for a fancy paste that tasted a lot like the liverwurst Mamma loved.

Victoria loathed the taste that asparagus left in her mouth. She was sickened by that gelatinous salmon mold.

What she would give for a meal of Limpin' Susan or Frogmore Stew. At times her mouth watered for a plate of rice and redeye gravy. Some days, oh, how she ached to be on Miss Abby's back steps with Binah and a bucket of steamed crabs—the two eating themselves silly, their mouths and hands dripping with butter and tasty crab juices, their bare feet swinging in the breeze.

"No bare feet." That was another of Miss Hardwick's rules. "Not even when you are in your bedroom."

Every night before slipping into bed Victoria had to rub her feet and hands with a strange concoction so much less lovely than Ma Clara's balm. Victoria then had to put her hands and feet in small muslin drawstring sacks.

Reading, writing, arithmetic. The proper way to sit, stand, talk, laugh, curtsy, hold opera glasses, retrieve a handkerchief from a purse, good topics of conversation, bad topics of conversation, how to sneeze, how to identify fine china, how to fashion her hair into a pompadour.

How to walk with purpose, how to stroll, how to hand a servant a calling card, how to—

Miss Hardwick's overriding, ultimate rule was this: "Whether you are out for a stroll or in the privacy of your boudoir, always conduct yourself as if you are being observed."

Then came the day when Miss Hardwick marched Victoria to the parlor, now crowded with trunks that had been delivered just that morning.

Miss Hardwick plucked dresses, skirts, and blouses from one trunk in particular.

"Arms out, please."

She piled clothes onto Victoria's outstretched arms.

She did the same with a few stunning gowns from a different trunk.

From the smallest trunk Miss Hardwick picked out several pairs of shoes. With those in hand she ordered Victoria to follow her up to the classroom, where she began to school her on what to wear when out walking, for a dinner party, for a picnic, when invited for tea, what to pack for a time in the country, what to . . .

Lessons, too, on fabrics, styles, and technical terms for different parts of an outfit. And Miss Hardwick now had Victoria reading *Godey's* fashion magazine with engravings of women smartly dressed, women who seemed very aware of being observed.

Victoria did enjoy playing dress-up, relished the challenge of choosing the right pair of shoes for such and such dress. Right purse. Right hat. What colors suited her best. Playing dress-up was the only sunshine in her lonely life.

And drawing her only comfort. When Miss Hardwick saw a sketch flutter to the floor from a book, on a piece of notepaper—"Not bad," she said with pursed lips. "You appear to possess some natural talent."

"As a child I enjoyed drawing in the sand," Victoria replied limply.

"You must hone this talent."

Two days later, Miss Hardwick gave Victoria a sketchbook with a black cloth spine and marbled wraps. A basic brown with yellow and green rivering, swirling around it. She also handed her a box of drawing sticks.

That bit of kindness was a lifeline.

* * *

During the time allotted for contemplation, after dinner, before she salved her hands and feet, then donned those muslin bags, Victoria sketched.

Trees from her dreams.

The moon.

Landscapes imagined.

Some days she peeked out her bedroom window and sketched from the street scene below. People passing to and fro. The wide woman scouring her steps. Leaves skipping down the street. Canada geese on a southbound journey.

One day she found herself sketching Ma Clara. She ripped out that page, balled it up, tossed it into the trash.

Victoria once thought there could be no greater loneliness than what she had known as a child when not around Ma Clara. Now she knew better.

Dorcas Vashon and Agnes Hardwick lectured her, tested her. But they never spoke to her, really. Never said anything such as, "My, don't you look lovely." Never asked how she liked the Regency Soup, Pheasant Sauté, or Snipe en Bellevue.

Whenever Victoria complimented Miss Graves on a dish, the woman looked away from her and Miss Hardwick gave her a stern look. The day Victoria, in a fit of pique, went down into the kitchen and asked Miss Graves if she could use any help, the woman flatly rebuffed her. Later came a scolding from Hardwick.

"You are to be pleasant to the help but never friendly.

You must understand that you live in one world and they in another."

A wider world?

Nagging headaches at the close of days.

Stomach upside down more often than not.

In the middle of the night Victoria sometimes awoke in a sweat, lingerings of nightmares swirling in her head.

A green dragon trying to pluck her eyes out.

A green phoenix grabbing her up by her hair.

Being crushed by a giant copy of *The Ladies' Book of Etiquette* as she walked out back at a moderate pace.

This had been the longest, the worst three months of her life. Some days she felt nothing but numb, dead inside. On one of those days, during contemplation time—

Home.

That was all Victoria could think about.

Home. She had been trying to work up the courage to tell Dorcas Vashon that she wanted to go home.

Victoria went over to her bureau and brought out the pouch in which she kept the money she had saved up.

She counted.

Two hundred and fifteen dollars and fifty-three cents.

Victoria practiced her speech: "Miss Dorcas, I am forever grateful to you for all that you have done for me, but I do not think I have what it takes to be a lady. There are simply too many rules and I doubt that I will ever master them all."

But what if Betty had worked out fine? Miss Abby didn't need three maids.

Well, then she'd ask Ma Clara to help her get cleaning work.

Every time Victoria screwed up her courage, she ended up backing down.

I think you have found favor with a good soul. You have been blessed, truly blessed.

Victoria had never known Ma Clara to be wrong about *anything.*

But could she have been wrong about Dorcas Vashon's offer?

Then came a day when Victoria got everything right—or almost right. Thoughts of returning to Forest City became vapors in the wind. But then in a moment of fatigue or amid a daydream or distraction she slurped her soup, took too large a mouthful of food, or tapped her three-minute egg a tad too hard—

Then came a Hardwick frown or scowl.

Victoria wept bitterly one day. "I'll never be a phoenix," she cried, "only the bird that burns."

A PEG-LEGGED MAN, DRUNKS, AND DUNG

There was a nip in the air, the chill of first frost. Feeling ten kinds of weary, too weary to even cry, Victoria stared blankly up at the white ceiling.

She glanced at the clock on her nightstand.

Thirty-eight more minutes of quiet contemplation.

"I simply cannot do this," she whispered. In a flash she was up and on her feet.

With the Griffin in the classroom and Dorcas Vashon taking a nap, Victoria saw her chance and took it.

She packed her Clapp's traveling bag, threw on a cloak, stuffed her pouch of money into a purse, then tiptoed downstairs. She turned the front doorknob slowly, knowing that it squeaked.

And the door creaked.

She froze, listened for footsteps. Hearing none, Victoria hurried out and onto the street.

On she walked in mincing steps as quickly as she could past tiny row houses, saloons, dreary shops, cottages, carters, hawkers, gaudy women wearing too much rouge, a peg-legged man, drunks, and dung.

When she stopped to catch her breath Victoria found herself before a lonesome-looking building. She looked up at its signs.

Port Mission.

Seamen's Reading Room.

She kept on in the direction that her nose told her would lead to the waterfront.

Victoria soon stopped again, realizing she had fled without a plan.

What if there is no ship sailing for Savannah today?

Then I will buy a ticket for the next one and get a room at a boardinghouse.

I do not even know how much a ticket costs.

How long might the wait be?

If days . . . Too, she reminded herself that she might not find work straightaway when she returned to Forest City. She would have to be very careful with her money. With that in mind, Victoria decided that if she did have to take a room while waiting for a ship to carry her home she would forgo meals at the boardinghouse. Instead she'd get herself some bread and cheese.

She stopped. *Get ahold of yourself! You will figure something out!*

Less panicked, Victoria walked on.

A few feet later she stopped again.

You look like you about to some way, somehow do us proud, Essie.

You make the most—the very most—of this here chance Dorcas Vashon is giving you.

"I am letting them all down," Victoria whispered. She chided herself, too, for being so spineless, for not having the courage to tell Dorcas Vashon that she quit. "I was just a waste of her time and money." Victoria looked at her cloak and thought about the clothing she had packed. Did that make her a thief?

No, she quickly reasoned. *I more than earned these things.* Anyway, once she reached Savannah she would write to Dorcas Vashon, explain everything to her, apologize.

Write to where? In fleeing, looking for an address or a street sign was the last thing on her mind.

Perhaps Miss Abby knew the address.

Head hung, Victoria began to weep. Not just about disappointing the folks back home and Dorcas Vashon. She was disappointed in herself. "Maybe a competent house girl is all I am meant to be," she mumbled.

"Hey, good-looking." A sly-looking sailor sidled over.

Victoria hurried on. She looked back every few seconds until she saw that sailor turn a corner. Then she slowed her pace.

And mourned.

She would never get another opportunity to rise in

life. She would never fulfill her dream of helping people who had it hard.

As Victoria walked on beneath a cloud-bedimmed sky something tugged at her mind. It was akin to a tap on the shoulder. As she wiped her eyes, it came to her.

"If there is no struggle, there is no progress," she whispered. "That is what Frederick Douglass has said."

If there is no struggle . . .

He was speaking in terms of the race rising.

There is no progress.

But did it not apply to her situation?

Victoria repeated Douglass's words again.

Again.

Again.

Each time she lifted her head a little higher.

She had taught herself with secondhand books and things from Miss Tansy's Odds-and-Ends Shop.

She had leapt at the opportunity to get out of that house on Minis Street.

She had read every book in Miss Abby's parlor.

She did now know the difference between a butter knife and a butter spreader.

She knew all about James Wormley's rise, about Orindatus Simon Bolívar Wall, and so many others.

She had gotten through *Bleak House*.

Victoria turned around, saw a frumpy colored woman approaching.

"Excuse me, ma'am."

The woman eyed her suspiciously. "Do I know you?"

"No, you do not, ma'am, but I am hoping that you can help me."

"How so?"

"Would you be so good as to tell me the way to Port Mission?"

Victoria was confident that if she could get to the mission she would be able to retrace her steps back to the house with first-floor shutters askew.

PHOENIX RISING

Victoria rose to—even relished—every challenge. When she made a blunder, she was no longer wounded by a Hardwick frown or scowl.

"I will do better next time," she said resolutely.

Whatever it takes! she constantly told herself. *Whatever it takes!*

More time walking around her bedroom with a book atop her head.

More time practicing the two-step, the waltz.

More time reading Webster's— *A-bāte'* ... *A-bў̆s'mal* ... *Ad'ju-tant* ... *Al'ba-trŏss* ... *As-sĭd'ū-oŭs-ly* ...

More time with Mrs. Beeton's book open to serviettes, mastering fancy napkin folding, from the Bishop and the Fan to the Mitre and the Lily.

More time ticking off all that she knew about the

Bruces, the Wormleys, the Syphaxes, the Murrays, Orindatus Simon Bolívar Wall . . .

Victoria plowed through stacks of old issues of the *Advocate* and of *Godey's* too:

"Visiting dress of purple plush and satin and plush damassé. . . . House dress of two shades of blue. The underskirt is of silk of the darkest shade, kilted. . . . Evening dress made of plain pink silk and striped satin. The underskirt is of the plain silk with a pleating around it, and fans of lace and pleated silk heading it. . . . Dinner dress of gendarme green silk. . . . Walking dress of two shades of elephant silk and camel's hair. . . ."

And Victoria indeed made *The Ladies' Book of Etiquette* her Bible.

"Do not pour coffee or tea from your cup into your saucer, and do not blow either these or soup. Wait until they cool. . . ."

"Use the butter-knife, salt-spoon, and sugar-tongs as scrupulously when alone, as if a room full of people were watching you. . . ."

"Wear a little of one bright color, if you will, but not more than one. . . ."

"A lady who desires to pay strict regard to etiquette, will not stop to gaze in at the shop windows. It looks countrified."

And there was the dictate that became Victoria's motto: "Never look back! It is excessively ill-bred."

Right! she said to herself. *I am a phoenix rising!*

I AM THE NIECE OF . . .

Dorcas Vashon, Miss Hardwick too. Both seemed strange that December morning during a breakfast of coddled eggs, toast, and tea. When Victoria spread a little too much butter on her toast neither woman made a remark. There wasn't even a cross look.

Victoria glanced at Miss Hardwick a time or two.

No cold stare, frown, or scowl. She did not look at all like a creature to be feared. She looked . . . soft.

Napkin off her lap and onto the table, Victoria rose. As always she was the first to leave the dining room so that Miss Hardwick could observe her posture, her gait.

Victoria was almost at the archway when Dorcas Vashon stopped her.

"Victoria, my dear."

Victoria turned around gracefully. "Yes, Miss Dorcas. Is there something that I can do for you?"

"Have a seat in the parlor, won't you? I will join you shortly."

Victoria passed the time in the parlor by taking an inventory of the room. She now had the language. The cloth fabric running across the draperies was a "valance." And this one was scalloped. The settee's fabric wasn't simply silk but "silk damask." The style of the parlor and dining room furniture was "Rococo Revival."

She had words for other things too.

Forcemeats.

Overmantel painting.

Roundabout conversation chair.

Marquetry.

The furniture legs she had likened to those of a ballerina on her toes were "cabriole legs." She had smiled when Miss Hardwick told her that the word was the French word for "caper" and also the name of a particular ballet leap. Victoria also now knew that "faille" was a type of ribbed silk fabric.

Dorcas Vashon had something behind her back when she entered the parlor.

"Eyes closed, my dear, hands out." There was a downright playfulness in her voice.

What Dorcas Vashon placed into Victoria's hands was small but had some weight.

Victoria opened her eyes to the most charming white onyx box. Engraved on the silver clasp—

A startled Victoria looked up at Dorcas Vashon. "I do not understand. You—you are giving me—" Victoria broke off, fighting back tears.

"Yes, my dear," replied Dorcas Vashon, honey in her voice.

Carefully Victoria opened the box, set it down on the table, took out one card. Against an off-white background in rich black ink—

Miss Victoria Vashon

She ran a finger over the raised lettering. "I don't know what to say. I am so very, very honored that you would . . ."

"And there is this, my dear." Dorcas Vashon handed her ward a black velvet pouch.

"How absolutely gorgeous!" Victoria gasped as she brought out a filigreed sterling silver calling card case.

That night, as Victoria sat at her dressing table preparing herself for bed, she stared at herself in the mirror. Again and again she whispered her new name. She felt stronger, felt victorious, felt . . .

"Victoria Vashon . . . Victoria Vashon . . . Victoria Vashon."

* * *

"Victoria Vashon is the niece of Dorcas Vashon of Charleston, South Carolina," began Miss Hardwick the next day. "Victoria Vashon is the daughter of Dorcas Vashon's late brother, Jeremiah."

Dorcas Vashon nodded as she stood in the schoolroom doorway. "I did have a younger brother and his name was Jeremiah." This was the one and only time Dorcas Vashon ever observed a lesson.

Miss Hardwick proceeded with more background: "It began with a woman named Dido Badaraka, a Moor, kidnapped in Morocco and soon bound for an auction block in Charleston. Dido was freed at about age twenty." Miss Hardwick lowered her head, shifted her feet. "After freedom Dido had three children with Baron Judah, a member of a prominent German-Jewish family. Their daughter Harriet made a life with a white man from England, Percy Vashon. He made a fortune as a cotton merchant, though, thankfully, he was not a slaveholder. Had the laws of South Carolina permitted, they would have married. Percy outlived Harriet, and when he died, his fortune went to their son Jeremiah and their daughter Dorcas."

"All true," said Dorcas Vashon. "As a young man my brother moved to New Orleans."

"And Jeremiah's wife?" asked Victoria. "Did he have other children?"

"Scarlet fever took his wife when it took him," said Dorcas Vashon. "And the story shall be this: You were their only child. You were spared their fate because as it so happened you had been sent to spend time with me in Charleston. Jeremiah's inheritance fell to me."

Victoria soaked it all in, feeling a fascination for Dido the Moor. *Othello* came to mind. She imagined Dorcas Vashon's grandmother a regal woman, the color of Ma Clara. Pictured her in a soft gold turban, a flowing robe of many colors.

"Let's repeat," said Miss Hardwick. "I will go slowly so that you can write it all down."

With breathless delight Victoria dipped her pen into the inkwell.

Miss Hardwick repeated the genealogy and all else she had said, then added this: "Due to several mysterious childhood illnesses in which you lingered in lethargy for long periods of time your education is a bit lacking. This is to explain why you speak no foreign language and play no musical instrument."

From a bag Victoria had never seen before Miss Hardwick brought out a stack of books. All about Charleston.

I am the niece of Dorcas Vashon . . . Dido Badaraka . . . Judah . . . from England . . . cotton merchant . . . lingering illness . . . no foreign language . . . no musical instrument . . . I am the niece of . . .

That was the day's only lesson.

"We leave in three weeks," Dorcas Vashon announced later that day, her face beaming. "And, by the way, Miss Hardwick will not be joining us."

"She will remain here?"

Dorcas Vashon shook her head. "She has another pupil to attend to. A young woman one of my lieutenants has taken from Macon to Philadelphia."

"Do you not have to be wherever Miss Hardwick is tutoring someone?"

"No, my dear, not always. She is perfectly capable of training young ladies without me. I am usually only in the picture when I come upon someone truly exceptional."

Victoria was speechless.

This was over a dinner of succotash and roasted potatoes, and for Victoria and Miss Hardwick, rack of lamb.

Lavish praise was served up too. Dorcas Vashon and Agnes Hardwick gushed over Victoria.

How far she had come.

How hard she had worked.

How quickly she learned—and learned from her mistakes.

"I am *extremely* proud of you," said Dorcas Vashon, with a glistening in her eyes.

For the first time ever Miss Hardwick's face bore a broad smile.

"We know that we have been quite severe," said Dorcas Vashon.

"We know that you have felt terribly lonely," Miss Hardwick practically cooed.

"But we did it for your own good," Dorcas Vashon

finished up. "To cultivate that habit of being reserved. To instill fortitude. To help you perfect your ability to persevere."

"Victoria," added Miss Hardwick, "if you can survive my training you can survive *anything*." She laughed. "Some girls have fled after just a few weeks."

"Remember the one—oh, her name escapes," said Dorcas Vashon. "The one who bolted after only three days."

"Annabelle," replied Miss Hardwick. "And did she not steal some silverware?"

"No, that was Maryanne," replied Dorcas Vashon. She turned to Victoria. "Not all of my picks have been perfect. On more than one occasion I have misjudged, saw more potential, more grit than was actually there."

"Victoria, how many times did you consider running away?" asked Miss Hardwick with a glance at Dorcas Vashon.

Victoria's eyes went from one woman to the other. *Do they know about that day?*

"Once," she finally said.

Victoria added a bit more mint jelly to her lamb. "Are they all—the ones who made it through—in Washington society?" she asked.

Dorcas Vashon shook her head, finished chewing a forkful of succotash. "They are spread abroad. Some in big cities. Others in small towns. And not all were positioned for society. Some I steered to be teachers. Quite a few I set up in business. Milliners . . . confectioners . . . dressmakers . . . You, my dear, are the first to be placed into Washington society. And the only one to bear my surname."

Victoria choked up. After composing herself, she asked, "And pray tell, Miss—Aunt Dorcas, how shall I do my part? How am I to help our people?"

"All in good time, dear. First we must get to the national capital." With that Dorcas Vashon helped herself to another forkful of succotash.

All the lessons, the reading, the times of contemplation, the moderate walking, the exercise, the practicing, practicing, practicing, all the days, weeks, months, it all came flooding back to Victoria. She could not recall the last time that she slurped her soup, spilled tea when pouring, fumbled with the sugar tongs, slouched, hunched, spoke as if she had marbles in her mouth.

"Perfect," Miss Hardwick had said earlier in the week of her omelet.

"Perfect," she had said two days ago of her recitation of "The Rime of the Ancient Mariner."

Things that once made Victoria's stomach ache, her temples throb had become reflex, instinct, easy like breathing.

A WIDER WORLD INDEED!

The national capital was light.

Lovely boulevards.

The January air crisp, clean.

"We will take a leisurely route to the house so that you may enjoy more sights." Dorcas Vashon had advised Victoria of this shortly before their train entered the Baltimore and Potomac Depot.

The railway station was a festival. Rich red brick, white stone trim. Victoria imagined its clock tower like a lighthouse from a distance. So taken with the structure she momentarily forgot that it was here that the nomadic Charles Guiteau, prone to rants and raves, put two bullets into President Garfield at close range.

"Gothic," she said under her breath.

"Yes, my dear, you are correct."

Gothic just like a huge building nearby.

"Center Market," said Dorcas Vashon. "I believe it is one of the largest markets in the nation."

"Miss Vashon?"

Old woman, young woman, both turned. Victoria lit up at the sight of such a distinguished-looking black man in livery, a belled top hat on his head. He bowed.

"Good day, Mr. Cordell Rodgers," responded Dorcas Vashon with a smile.

"At your service," replied Mr. Rodgers. He reached for the luggage a porter had neatly stacked beside them.

With the luggage taken care of, Mr. Rodgers escorted them over to a shiny black two-horse brougham. Victoria felt a little breathless as Mr. Rodgers helped her into the carriage, immaculate inside. Now this was more like her daydreams.

"When I last telegraphed Mr. Rodgers I told him to surprise us on the route," said Dorcas Vashon as the carriage began to move.

Past Sixth Street Park, past Third Street Park, past the stunning—

"Botanic gardens," said Dorcas Vashon.

Victoria had read of a particular climbing plant making fifty-foot-long shoots and producing two-foot-long racemes of flowers. Bold blue petals. Calyxes scarlet.

Next the carriage pulled up to—

"The Capitol," said Victoria in a hushed tone. Pictures in books and magazines did not do it justice. "A palace," she added.

"And up top is . . . ?"

"The Statue of Freedom designed by a white man, but it was one of our own, Philip Reid, who supervised its casting."

"Indeed."

On Rodgers drove, up Indiana, pausing before Judiciary Square, then he turned the carriage around, traveled north, and soon came to another halt.

"It looks like a castle or a cathedral," said Victoria, delighting in the National Museum with its arched windows, warm rich brick and tile facade. She counted its spires, wondered what the floor was like beneath its rotunda.

Even more castle-like was the next building they passed.

"The Smithsonian Institution," Victoria whispered. "What a mighty fortress."

Next, the President's Park, the President's House. Victoria thought there was something lonely about that big white house. It looked rather different than it did in engravings Dorcas Vashon and Miss Hardwick had shown her.

"See to your left in the distance, the building under construction? It will house the departments of War, Navy, and State."

Next came Lafayette Square and nearby—

"This, my dear, is Wormley's Hotel."

Victoria hoped that on another day she would be treated to at least a peek inside this stately building with over fifty bedrooms, a large parlor, large dining room, large kitchen too. She had also read that the rooms were outfitted with the finest of fine furniture. There were Brussels carpets and Smyrna rugs.

"James Wormley started out as a hackney coachman like his father, yes?"

"That is right, my dear."

Victoria summoned up more information. "His wife had a confectionary, and he had a catering business next door to her shop. He later opened up a restaurant and he owned several boardinghouses. He studied cookery in Paris."

"Correct again, my dear."

"And it was here back in 1877, when the presidential election was in dispute, that a group of Republican and Democratic politicians made a deal. Rutherford B. Hayes would get the presidency if he agreed to remove the remaining federal troops from the South."

"Yes, the Corrupt Bargain. The Great Betrayal."

"Did Wormley know what those men were doing?"

"I would like to think not."

"I can only imagine how marvelous it is to dine there," said Victoria as the carriage moved on.

"I am sure that you will find out for yourself one day."

Victoria puzzled. "You mean . . . I thought—"

"Wormley's is for anyone who can pay his prices. The color line is not as pronounced here as elsewhere in the South. We can, for example, sit anywhere we wish on the streetcars, stay in any hotel we can afford, attend any theater."

Soaking in the sights of the national capital, Victoria engaged in no gasping, no oohing and aahing, made no quick turns of the head. She sat primly in her heliotrope dress beneath a lightweight coat and with her hands nestled in off-white beaded gloves. Victoria sat erectly, as if aware that she was being observed.

Neither did Victoria lose her composure when the carriage pulled up to a stunning house.

A wider world indeed!

SECOND FLOOR FRONT

"Splendid!" said Dorcas Vashon.

Mr. Rodgers had just helped her from the carriage.

"Mr. Rodgers, you have done very well indeed. This is even more exquisite than I imagined."

This time the basement windows registered right away with Victoria. Larger, higher than the ones in that house in Baltimore. Above the basement windows was a white stone projecting bay window. To its right and up five slate-gray steps, double doors with decorative molding.

Triple windows on the second floor. Tall windows with ornamental hooding, two of them over the balcony that was the top of the bay window.

Triple windows on the third floor too. Dormer windows framed by scalloped slate.

Victoria knew that the third floor was no small attic space. The house's mansard roof told her that the third floor was a spacious place. Though only three stories the house was soaring.

Victoria and Dorcas Vashon were midway up the walkway when the front door opened.

"Welcome, Miss Dorcas, Miss Victoria," said a middleaged woman with friendly eyes. She wore a crisp black dress beneath a snow-white pinafore. Her cap was snow white too.

"Victoria, this is Millicent Rodgers."

Victoria soon learned that Mr. and Mrs. Rodgers were livein servants, occupying the top floor. The Mrs. served as cook, housekeeper, laundress. The Mr. as coachman, butler, and his wife's all-around helping hand in this house of marble fireplaces, parquet floors, and light streaming into every room. The furniture was even finer than in that house in Baltimore. In addition to a parlor there was also a sitting room on the first floor.

And this time Victoria's bedroom was second floor front. As she looked around the room . . .

White wood furniture, from bedstead to nightstand to dressing table and desk . . .

Teal-blue wallpaper with pink and white roses . . .

Shining oak floors . . .

Off-white rug beneath her bed . . .

Off-white lace curtains . . .

Victoria felt even more like a Cinderella than she had in that fancy black mourning dress.

Thou God seest me.

"You did and I thank you," Victoria whispered later that night, sitting at her dressing table, brushing her hair, envisioning magnificent tomorrows.

CHARMED!

Out. Victoria relished being able to be out and about. Walks in parks. Walks up and down Pennsylvania Avenue. Walks to Howard University. In a coat and muffler on chilly days. In a cape and gloves when warmer. There were carriage rides too. Like the walks, at the start never without Dorcas Vashon as chaperone.

One early walk was to 1109 F Street, NW, home of Samuel Estren, wigmaker, his wife, Louisa, a hairdresser, their three young children, and Gertrude King, the family's young servant, who cheerfully brought tea and sandwiches into the parlor within a few minutes of their arrival. But the purpose of the visit went beyond socializing.

Within about thirty minutes a woman who inspired awe entered the parlor.

"Dorcas Vashon, Victoria Vashon," said Mrs. Estren, "I present Madame Elizabeth Keckley."

Victoria only learned of the woman when they were en route to the Estrens'. The day before Dorcas Vashon had only told her that on the morrow they would visit a dressmaker.

"She is Virginia-born," Dorcas Vashon began as they exited the house with the mansard roof. "She spent thirty years in slavery, until she finally had sufficient money to purchase her freedom. She went on to become one of the most sought-after dressmakers in the nation." Dorcas Vashon paused. "She was modiste to none other than Mary Todd Lincoln. After Mrs. Lincoln became her customer, well, flocks of white society women just had to have dresses designed by Madame Keckley."

By then they were on N Street. Victoria stopped. "Do you mean to tell me, Miss Dorcas—I mean Aunt Dorcas— that a woman who made clothes for a *president's wife*, for *white society women* will make clothes for *me*?"

"Why, yes, my dear. You are just as worthy. Now come along." After a few more steps Dorcas Vashon continued. "She had a busy shop on 12th Street; at one point she employed about twenty women. But then after the war, she wrote her memoirs, *Behind the Scenes*."

Me? That was all Victoria could think.

"It was all feathers and furs after that," said Dorcas Vashon, voice lowered. "Mrs. Lincoln and other white women believed that Madame Keckley had overstepped, revealed too much about Mrs. Lincoln and their private conversations. They punished her by taking their business elsewhere. And so I want to make a point of providing her with some work. She deserves it, doubly so given the great work she did here for our people during the war."

"Was she a nurse or a . . . ?"

Dorcas Vashon shook her head. "When the national capital bulged with thousands of our people who had escaped slavery—contrabands they were called, most from Maryland and Virginia. Anyway, Madame Keckley organized the Contraband Relief Association. She helped raise thousands of dollars for those destitute people, money for food, clothing, medicine. She worked hand in hand with James Wormley."

With her white hair swept up, her perfect posture, perfect poise, Madame Elizabeth Keckley was a queen.

"Fine bones," she said when she had Victoria up in her workshop. "Excellent proportions." As Madame Keckley continued to size her up, Victoria felt no awkwardness, no fear as on the day of Miss Hardwick's arrival. Victoria was thoroughly at ease with being observed.

"I have a lovely emerald satin that is ideal for you. It will most definitely complement your eyes. Oh, what ideas you inspire—from day dresses to the fancy!"

*   *   *

Victoria was surprised at how quickly word of their arrival spread. Mrs. Fitzhugh, a slender woman with a high fore-head and upturned nose, was the first one to call on them.

"Washington is a very small town," Dorcas explained after the woman left.

Mrs. Miller came next.

Then Mrs. Tyler, Mrs. Taylor, Mrs. Tilghman. Mrs. . . .

Soon, in chiffons, taffetas, failles, moirés, and silk- and cotton-backed satins Victoria attended teas, luncheons, recitals. She met Syphaxes, Greens, Cooks.

Early on she said little other than "Pleased to meet you" and such. She was not so much sheepish as in absolute awe. To have read about these people was one thing; to see them in the flesh . . .

Former US Senator Blanche K. Bruce was more hand-some in real life than in photographs. "He was born in slavery," she said to herself, "and now he lives in a courtly home on M Street."

Orindatus Simon Bolívar Wall looked as intense and powerful as his hefty name. Victoria had been a bit ner-vous when meeting him. He had lived in Charleston for a time. What if he asked questions?

"Charmed!" he had said when introductions were made at a dinner at the Andersons'. Then with a click of his heels he went on his way.

"Another one," Victoria said to herself, bursting with pride. "Slave . . . first colored man made a captain in the Union army . . . lawyer."

Victoria wondered how she might be a credit to the race as she and Dorcas Vashon left a recital at the Tilghmans'. *I must contribute! I must say thank you for this blessing of a wider world!*

OF MEETING MOLLIE CHURCH

"And how do you find Washington?" asked Fanny Miller during the first tea Dorcas Vashon had Victoria host. Fanny was a petite girl with long raven hair. Her father was a pharmacist and owned a fair amount of real estate.

Victoria poured. "I find Washington quite grand, quite wonderful. Were you all born here?" Victoria had decided at the outset that during her early days in society she would steer conversations away from herself as much as possible.

"Yes, we were all born and bred here," replied Penelope Fitzhugh, a dour freckle-faced girl with auburn hair. Her parents owned a thriving catering business.

"And the Mrs. came to the marriage with some family money," Dorcas Vashon had told Victoria.

"Yes, indeed, all born and bred right here" added short, pudgy Clementine Tyler, daughter of a dentist who had inherited two barber shops that catered to only prominent and prosperous white men.

"I have never been to Charleston," said Penelope. "Tell me, what is it like?"

This was on a different day. The girls were at Penelope's townhouse, in the sitting room playing hearts.

"Well, the word that most people use to describe Charleston is 'charming' and that it is," replied Victoria.

Clubs lead. Having none Victoria seized the opportunity to shed the king of spades.

"What made your aunt want to relocate?" asked Fanny.

"She simply wanted a change," replied Victoria.

"So Washington will be your new home?"

"That has yet to be decided. This is why Aunt Dorcas has only rented the house."

After Fanny won that hand Victoria asked, "What shall we play next?"

"I vote for whist," chirped Clementine.

As Clementine shuffled, Fanny dished out gossip: who was seen awfully cozy in a cafe with a woman not his wife; how Mrs. Richardson really got that black eye; who had a little too much to drink at the Men of Mark banquet.

"I hear that Mollie Church may pay our city another visit soon," said Penelope after cards were dealt.

"Oh. Not *her*!" shrieked Fanny. "Our young men will be beside themselves."

Victoria looked up from her hand. "Who is this Mollie . . . ?"

"Church. Mollie Church," replied Fanny.

"She is the daughter of the richest colored man in the South, Robert Church," Clementine explained. "I believe most of his wealth derives from real estate."

Fanny leaned in. "I have heard that not all of his holdings are, well, respectable. If you know what I mean?"

"What *do* you mean?" asked Penelope.

"They say he owns saloons along with—" Fanny leaned in again. "Houses of ill-repute."

Victoria flinched. "So his daughter, Mollie Church, she is very beautiful I take it."

"Yes, very," said Clementine. "She was the talk of the town last March. The Bruces invited her up to attend President Garfield's inauguration. She was escorted in by Frederick Douglass."

"How does she know the Bruces?" asked Penelope, popping a lemon bonbon into her mouth.

"Mr. Bruce and her father are good friends," replied Fanny.

"You all sound as if you do not much care for this Mollie Church," said Victoria.

"I would not say that," Penelope began. "It is just that—"

"She is a little too serious," said Clementine. "I heard that her great ambition is to earn a bachelor's degree *and* a master's degree at Oberlin College. She is now attending its preparatory school."

Fanny smirked. "I have heard that she intends to major in, of all things, Greek and Latin."

"What is so wrong with that?" asked Victoria.

"Unnatural. Those are *men's* courses!" said Fanny, pursing her lips. "She will never find a husband if she pursues a man's course."

"But she is beautiful and rich," countered Clementine.

Victoria was so relieved when the chatter ceased and they got on with their game of whist.

Greek and Latin...How interesting. On her way home Victoria daydreamed of meeting Mollie Church.

THEN STOOD THERE IN A DAZE

"What say you, Aunt Dorcas? The cobalt-blue, floral silk crepe de chine jacket with a tailored front peplum over the ivory skirt or . . ."

She rattled off three other outfits.

"My dear, you look divine in whatever you wear."

On that late March day Victoria was ecstatic about tomorrow. She wanted to look her best, her absolute best, when she entered Metropolitan AME Church's Bethel Hall for its literary society's weekly lecture.

In the end she decided on the cobalt blue.

"Not to fan the flame of sectional animosity now happily in the process of rapid and I hope permanent extinction . . ."

Victoria never knew that he was so tall.

". . . not to recount the long list of wrongs, inflicted on

my race during more than two hundred years of merciless bondage..."

His voice was deep, full of power, akin to a command from God.

His mane of hair, mustache, beard were on their way to snow white. But he did not look old, oh, no. Strong, sturdy. And so immaculately dressed in a stark white shirt, jet-black suit, black cravat at his neck.

The Honorable Frederick Douglass was truly magnetic, majestic.

"...nor yet to draw, from the labyrinths of far-off centuries, incidents and achievements wherewith to rouse your passions, and enkindle your enthusiasm, but to pay a just debt long due, to vindicate in some degree a great historical character, of our own time and country, one with whom I was myself well acquainted, and whose friendship and confidence it was my good fortune to share..."

His subject was John Brown.

Victoria looked around discreetly, hoping to catch a glimpse of Daniel Murray and his wife, Anna, for Dorcas Vashon had told her that an uncle of Anna's, Lewis Sheridan Leary, and her cousin John Copeland had been among the five black men who took part in John Brown's failed raid on the arsenal at Harper's Ferry, a raid meant to spark a mighty uprising against slavery.

When Frederick Douglass finished, the applause was

thunderous, the crowd on its feet. Victoria clapped hard. But ladylike.

Later, at the reception, she was a bird afraid to fly.

There she stood a mere eight, maybe ten feet away from him.

Dorcas Vashon was mingling. Victoria was on her own.

What should she—what could she say or ask the great man? Victoria thought quickly. Back in Baltimore she had read her hero's latest autobiography. Perhaps she could compliment him on that book. While she hesitated, the men and women with whom Douglass had been chatting peeled away. There he was alone, serving himself some punch. It was now or never.

Victoria walked over. "Mr. Douglass . . ."

He looked up, smiled. "Yes?"

"My name is Victoria Vashon." She curtsied, extended her hand. "I am the niece of Dorcas Vashon of Charleston, South Carolina."

His hand swallowed hers up.

"I—I—" Touching his hand, standing there beneath his commanding gaze left Victoria momentarily tongue-tied. She cleared her throat. "Your autobiographies have been such an inspiration."

"Why, thank you . . . Beg pardon, your name again?"

"Vashon. Victoria Vashon."

"I am glad to have been of service."

"They have been my compass point and guide."

She so badly wanted to tell him the role his life played in her decision to say yes to Dorcas Vashon's offer. Wanted to tell him how nine of his words lifted her up when she hit rock bottom.

He set his cup on the table. "Where are my manners? Would you care for some punch?"

The Honorable Frederick Douglass serve *her*? Even if she were thirsty she would have declined for fear of trembling hands. "No thank you, sir."

"And tell me, Miss Vashon, how long have you been in our city?"

"We have only been here for a few weeks."

"You said you are from . . . ?"

"Charleston."

"Oh, Frederick!" an elderly lady with a cane called out from across the room. "Oh, Frederick!" She waved her white handkerchief in the air, then hobbled over and grabbed his arm.

"Will you excuse me, Miss Vashon?" He bowed.

"Of course, sir." Victoria curtsied, then stood there in a daze.

If that were not enough, weeks later she was at the great man's house!

INVENTING VICTORIA

"Mr. Douglass is out of town lecturing," said Dorcas Vashon when she told Victoria about the upcoming event. "His sons are hosting the Monday Night Literary Club. The speaker will be Henry E. Baker. His subject will be 'Originality.'"

Victoria was disappointed that she wouldn't see the great man again, but the prospect of being in his home had her in high delight.

"Baker is a recent graduate of Howard's law school," Dorcas Vashon informed Victoria as the carriage pulled up to Cedar Hill. "Top of his class he was. He works at the patent office. As I understand it, he is at work on a book about colored inventors."

"*Colored inventors?*" Not in her lessons, not in a newspaper, nor in any book had Victoria learned of colored people inventing anything.

"Yes, my dear. People like the tailor Thomas Jennings

of New York City. Fifty, sixty years ago he invented a method of cleaning clothes without the use of water. 'Dry scouring,' he called it. What we today call dry cleaning."

Victoria smiled wide. "It never ends, does it?"

"What?"

"Learning."

"Not if you are awake to the world."

They were nearly at Douglass's front door.

"If only Mr. Baker knew," Dorcas Vashon added, "he might have a chapter in his book titled 'Inventing Victoria.'"

Victoria smiled as they stepped inside Frederick Douglass's hilltop house with his splendid view of the national capital.

"Now there ought not to be anything strange or unbelievable in the fact that in any given group of more than 10,000,000 human beings, of whatever race, living in our age, in our country, and developing under our laws, one can find multipled examples of every mental bent."

Hear! Hear! thought Victoria as Baker lamented that so many people outside the race had "the fixed conviction that no colored man has any well-defined power of initiative, that the colored man has no originality of thought . . ."

* * *

Why not? Victoria thought after the lecture. She drifted away from the East Parlor mingling. "Where is the library?" she asked one of the waitresses. Claire Branch had told Victoria that Douglass's library was a sight to behold.

It was indeed. Its walls were hung with portraits of John Brown and a host of other famous people, some colored, some white. Most intriguing was an engraving of someone Victoria did not know.

A determined black man with so much purpose in his eyes.

Dressed in something like a toga.

A staff in his left hand.

Beneath his portrait was written *Cinque*

Below that: *The Chief of the Amistad Captives.*

Victoria made a mental note to find out who he was.

Beholding Douglass's rolltop desk . . .

Letter sorter.

Paper cutter.

Blotter.

Inkstand and pen.

Victoria imagined the great man deep in thought, writing his speeches.

And the books! "Must be more than a thousand books in here," she whispered as she looked around the room.

Slave Songs of the United States . . . Socrates, Plato & the

Grecian Sophists…Lake Ngam…Narrative of William Brown, a Fugitive Slave…The Negro in the American Rebellion, His Heroism & His Fidelity…Buds and Blossoms from Our Own Garden…Moral Heroism; Or, the Trials and Triumphs of the Great and Good…The Complete Poetical Works of Robert Burns…Complete Works of William Shakespeare…The Odyssey of Homer…Looking Backward. He had two copies of the *Columbian Orator.*

"How much I would have missed out on!" Victoria whispered, reflecting on that mad moment in Baltimore when she fled the house with first-floor shutters askew.

How much I would have missed out on! she thought again during Madame Selika's concert at Lincoln Hall. As she listened to the "Queen of Staccato," so resplendent in her soft pink gown, Victoria wondered what the prima donna had worn when she sang at the White House. The first colored person to do so, she had read. Selika's "Ave Maria" moved Victoria to tears. She also wept during a performance by the Fisk Jubilee Singers at First Congregational.

Then came the grand masquerade at Tallmadge Hall, where Victoria nibbled on croùtes de foie gras, mushrooms au gratin, and asparagus on toast, sipped champagne, swirled, twirled, glided among harlequins, dukes, knights, princes, Greek gods, an Indian chief, an Ali Baba, a mermaid, an Alice in Wonderland.

It was more than she could have dreamed of.

"What an ingenious costume!"

"Did you come up with this?"

"You look marvelous!"

The compliments overflowed and overwhelmed. Victoria had designed her costume herself with help from Madame Keckley: a petticoat of pale gold satin with an overdress made entirely of peacock feather tips and eyes and with a laced-up back. Victoria's gilded Venetian mask, studded with glass beads of many colors, sported a peacock feather on one side.

When someone asked, "Why peacock feathers?" Victoria replied simply, "Renewal."

She sat not one dance out.

If only the Sarah Paces of the world could see me now!

GREATER EXPECTATIONS

She had just finished a portrait of a lady. The woman had high cheekbones. Hair in a high pompadour with bangs. A haughty gaze. Across the top Victoria wrote, "What Now?"

As the weather warmed there was badminton, lawn tennis, archery, croquet. She mastered them rather quickly.

What now?

More teas. More card parties. More needlework sessions.

What now?

Victoria began to chide herself for getting so caught up. Just as on that Baltimore street, she was disappointed in herself. There was a term for what she was on the verge of becoming.

Social butterfly.

That's not who she wanted to be.

But wait a minute. She hadn't gotten *that* caught up. Had she, she would not now be weary of the put-on smiles, weary of the vacuous chatter, gossip, weary of pretending to be oblivious to the whispers.

"I have heard that Dorcas Vashon will leave the girl her entire fortune."

"I hear that she speaks no French."

"Are they related to George Boyer Vashon, who taught at Howard some years ago?"

"She is quite a lovely little thing."

Weary of Fanny constantly carping about some colored person who embarrassed her. A charwoman talking too loud in the street to "another old crone." Folks who left home without combing their hair. Women wearing red bandannas. People who hung their heads out of windows.

Gauche, Victoria said to herself, then allowed a wry smile.

Another day Fanny fumed over a doddering old man reeking of himself who tapped her on the shoulder and asked, "Where the poorhouse at?"

"The audacity of some of these gutter people!" Fanny huffed.

Victoria cringed at Fanny's cruelty as she sat in the Miller sitting room doing needlepoint.

"People like that are the reason why our kind of people may very well stop attending Emancipation Day."

Back in March Victoria had feasted on news about plans for the upcoming celebration of the twentieth anniversary of the end of slavery in the District of Columbia. When that April day came . . .

All those colored men in such regalia. Sashes and braiding. Hats festooned.

Spotless black carriages bearing Richard Greener and other honored guests.

On and on the parade went.

The Knights of Moses . . . the Galilean Fishermen . . . The Eastern Star Twilight Cadets . . . the Lively Eight . . . the Good Samaritans.

"Oh, look!" Victoria had gasped when she spotted the chariots decorated with flags and bunting. There were two young women dressed like queens. In one sat—

"That's Albertina Miller," sniffed Penelope. "She has always been quite stuck on herself. She is no relation to Fanny, by the way."

In the other chariot sat—

"That is Ruth Ward," said Penelope. "She is ghastly and as dumb as a brick."

Yes, Penelope Fitzhugh, tatting a lace collar, liked to tear people down too. She pointed out who wore the same dress twice in one week. "She is big and black—who would want that?" Penelope once said of the Cox girl, only twelve.

"We only went to this year's Emancipation Day parade for your sake, what with you being new to the city," said Fanny. Months later she was still talking about how embarrassed to the bone she was over the way some colored people conducted themselves, onlookers and regular folks who marched behind the mounted marshals, honored guests, fraternal organizations, and chariots. "Remember that old hag kicking up her heels and hollering so."

"And what about those raggedy, drunken men!" said Penelope. "There should be a law that only people in their Sunday best can march in the parade."

"Well, perhaps those people were slaves," said Victoria. "Surely the day must have a powerful hold on such people, more so than on people born free." Victoria seethed at the thought of the cutting remarks Fanny and the others would make about Ma Clara, Miss Abby, Old Man Boney, ferryman Jack. She could hear them calling Binah a dunce, making fun of the way she talked. Victoria thought back to how people like Florence and Drusilla Pace looked down on the likes of her and Primus Grady.

Clementine Tyler was not with them during that needle-point session at the Millers'. Victoria was certain that if she were, all Clementine would do is natter incessantly about the latest in buttons and bows.

The death of Longfellow, Roman remains found in London, the goings-on in government—Victoria could not recall meaningful conversations with Clementine, Penelope, and Fanny. When she tried to change the subject from buttons and bows or "gutter people," they simply humored her for a few minutes, then steered the conversation back to something vapid. Or cruel.

Things were a bit better when Claire Branch joined them for tea, cards, or needlework. Claire, chocolate, cheery, and dimple-chinned, the daughter of a professor of literature at Howard, had a keen and hungry mind. During interludes she and Victoria often talked themselves to pieces over current events, *The Prince and the Pauper*, or some other book they had recently read. Claire was among the few young women Victoria met who did not put on excessive airs. The folks back home would like her. That thought sent Victoria wondering if Betty was being a good friend to Binah.

Victoria hoped to see as much as possible of Claire in coming months, before she got married, after which Claire would spend less and less time with single young ladies.

And so many of the young men, Victoria found them insufferable.

Timothy Fitzhugh with his high forehead and vulture eyes got a little too close when he was teaching her archery at one of his family's lawn parties.

Flemming Cary—egad!—what a dandy, what a hungry wolf grin. He boasted endlessly about his family's summer home on the Chesapeake Bay. "No one who is anyone stays in the city throughout the entire summer," he informed Victoria one day.

The way the young men eyed her, sniffed around her,

made Victoria sick, as did the competition for a first dance, who was first to bring her a cup of punch, who could corner her the longest in chitchat.

Jonah Galloway was one exception. A few years older than the others, a bit sheepish, with kind eyes, Jonah never strutted about or pushed himself forward. With his Deep South accent akin to hers, Victoria warmed to him. Also because he seemed ill at ease in society. And there was his candor too.

"It has taken me some time to get through Howard," Jonah told her at a Capitol Guard reception, "because I came up through slavery and did not avail myself of learning to read and write on the sly when I had the chance. But I am bound and determined. If the Good Lord permits I will press on to Howard's medical school."

"Good for you!" responded Victoria.

"I am especially interested in cures for the cold and chills."

On another occasion, when Jonah mentioned that he had been on Sherman's March, he told her about the white man whose surname he took, the man he followed all the way to the capital. Victoria ached to ask him questions about the march but decided against it, just continued to wonder if he had known Mamma.

Conversations with Jonah factored into Victoria's yearning for great expectations. Not of life but of herself.

Clear about the importance of keeping up appearances,

Victoria nevertheless found clever ways to decline more and more invitations.

She spent more time inside that house with the mansard roof or in a park sketching. A time or two she had an urge to sketch people and places in Forest City, but then felt rebuked by the *Ladies' Book of Etiquette*.

"Never look back! It is excessively ill-bred."

PROCTOR'S RESORT

"Back in Savannah you said that you could make me into someone who could help a lot of our people."

After breakfast Victoria and Dorcas Vashon had retired to the sitting room.

"While I have been having a marvelous time, I fail to see how going to teas and dances, playing parlor games and such does anything for our people. In fact so many of colored society do not seem to care about the lowly."

The roses were in stunning display on this early June morning.

"They care as they can," responded Dorcas Vashon. "They have charities for the needy." After a pause she added, "Patience, my dear. One does not barge into society. You are still a newcomer, an outsider. Give it time. Wait until you are invited to join this committee or that. Your time will come."

May it come soon, Victoria thought. "Aunt Dorcas, there is something else."

"Yes?"

"Why were you so keen on my becoming friends with Fanny, Penelope, and Clementine? They are rather obnoxious."

"It was another test of sorts."

"A test?"

Dorcas Vashon nodded.

"A test of what?"

"Have you become obnoxious?"

Victoria laughed. "No, thank goodness, I have not!"

"Bravo!" Dorcas Vashon then changed the subject. "Peruse the *Advocate* and decide where we shall spend some of the summer?"

There was Myrtle Hall in Harper's Ferry, West Virginia, operated by a Mrs. W. B. Evans. A Mrs. Neal had a board-inghouse in Old Point Comfort, Virginia. Those ads left Victoria cold but not an item about a place in Rockville, Maryland.

"Mr. Samuel Proctor has added to his Rockville home addition rooms sufficient to accommodate 30 persons," said the *Advocate* of a house that stood high upon a hill. It boasted an exquisite view of the surrounding countryside, a cool spring, and a fine lawn, perfect for archery and croquet.

Victoria circled the article, showed it to Dorcas Vashon later that day.

"Proctor's Resort," said Dorcas Vashon, skimming the item. "I have heard very good things about that place."

Proctor's Resort it was.

The sixteen-mile, one-hour B&O train ride to Rockville—past fields, past cows chewing the cud, past laborers swinging scythes—was delightful. So too the half-hour carriage ride from the depot up to the Proctors' huge clapboard house with a wide wraparound veranda.

They arrived near dusk, greeted by evergreen Chinese lanterns and hooded candles on the lawn. And by Samuel and Alice Proctors' warm smiles.

There were only ten other guests at the time, none of whom Victoria or Dorcas Vashon knew. And Victoria would not have it any other way. What a relief it was to be far away from society, from gossip, from boasts and brags.

Then he came.

PURPOSE IN HIS EYES

He was a long, cold drink of water on a parching day.

Victoria had seen him once, at a Fitzhugh soiree.

"Who is he?" she had nonchalantly asked Fanny of the tall, angular young man with a razor-sharp mustache and purpose in his eyes.

"Oh, that is Adgerton Mott's nephew," replied Fanny.

"Can't be!" gasped Clementine.

"Why not?" asked Victoria.

"Adgerton Mott could pass for white if he wanted to. That young man is black as coal."

"He is Mr. Mott's nephew by marriage," said Fanny, "not by blood."

That was another thing that vexed Victoria. So much talk about color. Light skin was cause for pride for so many, whereas it had always been a source of shame for her.

While Victoria chanced glances at the tall young man

with purpose in his eyes, Clementine asked her if she were as light as Adgerton Mott would she pass. "Some of my mother's people," the chatterbox went on to say, "moved to Massachusetts and became white. No doubt they live in fear of one of us seeking them out and letting the truth be known."

Victoria froze. What if someone from Savannah came to Washington, someone who knew her, knew that she was passing, as someone born into a good family as opposed to the daughter of a—

Victoria stifled her anxiety by carrying on with the conversation. "Why would I want to pass for white?"

Clementine's mouth fell open. "You would have such an easier life!"

"After all that they have done to our people?" Victoria then steered the conversation back to him. "Does he live in the capital?"

"No, he is from New York City," Fanny informed her. "His mother—no, his father recently died and left him some money. Not a lot by any means."

"His name?" Victoria asked, taking pains not to look his way.

AND ONE DAY A KISS

"Name's Wyatt, Wyatt Riddle." He tipped his straw boater.

Victoria was sketching on the Proctor's back veranda when he strode into view wearing beige linen pants and an open-collar white shirt. A windowpane-check jacket was slung over a shoulder.

"Victoria Vashon. Pleased to meet you." She gave him a small smile, felt a quickening.

He bowed, shook her hand, kissed it. "Pleased to meet you."

"You have just arrived?"

"Last night."

"We did not see you at dinner."

"I arrived quite late due to a train delay."

Victoria, feeling nervous, strange, just smiled, then returned to her sketch pad. Out of the corner of her eye she watched him taking in the view.

"I swear this place is like a peek at heaven."

"Indeed. It is such a lovely spot."

Wyatt turned around, leaned on the bright-white railing. She could feel him staring at her.

She wondered what he was thinking as she continued sketching, determined to be the picture of poise in her lightweight white cotton eyelet day dress with three-quarter-length sleeves. She loved that dress with its stand-up collar and tiny vertical pleats on the shoulder yoke as well as below the waist and around the hip. With its flowing skirt, such an easy dress to move in. It always made her feel cool, like a cloud.

"Do you mind if I join you?" he asked.

"Not at all." There was a fluttering in her stomach as he sat in the white wicker chair next to hers.

He stretched his arms, rubbed his hands. "May I see?" He pointed at her sketch pad.

She handed him the pad. "I am not very good, it is just something—"

He looked out at the rolling billows of blue-gray mountain ridges, then down at the drawing. "I am certainly no expert on art, but it seems to me that you have quite captured the mood. The clearness. The serenity." He looked from the sketch to her. "The beauty."

Victoria found herself staring at his hands. "Capable" came to mind.

"How long are you staying?"

"Just for a week. Then I will be returning home."

Victoria feigned ignorance. "Oh, and where is home?"

"New York City."

She could feel him staring at her again as she added a broad-winged hawk to her mountainscape.

The day had begun in mist. After breakfast Victoria had gone for a stroll, all the while thinking about purpose, wondering when, how she could be of service to her people. Before she and Dorcas Vashon arrived at Proctor's Resort she had read a frightful article about colored living in squalid alley dwellings, where children went about half-naked and died at an alarming rate. She had not seen that aspect of Washington.

"What will you tackle next?" asked Wyatt after Victoria added the hawk.

"I do not know as of yet. My aunt and I only arrived in the capital several months ago. I have not yet—"

"I meant, what will you draw next?"

Silly goose. "Oh, I don't know . . ." She pointed east. "Perhaps that stunning cedar."

With the ebb and flow of small talk, with Wyatt's ease with silence, Victoria became convinced, as she savored the sun and crystalline air, that Wyatt was no ordinary man, especially after he astonished her with this question: "Would you do me the honor of having dinner with me tonight? Just the two of us. Out here on the veranda."

She was taken aback, yes, but at the same time deliciously thrilled. His straightforwardness was refreshing, attractive. He did not hem and haw. Seemed to have no weasel ways. He was clearly well-bred, but—

There was something different about him. He did not care to impress and was not easily impressed or amused. Definitely he was not the type to suffer fools gladly.

"I will need to check with my aunt," Victoria finally said.

Their solo dinner on the veranda, sweetened by soft breezes, led to more back veranda talk, to walks in the woods and to the spring, led to a picnic and one day a kiss.

Hand in hand they had toured Proctor's garden with its melons, tomato plants, pole beans, walking onions, and herbs. They had strolled through nearby woods. They had idled in a patch overrun by anemones, bluebells, oxeye daisies, and a host of other wildflowers. Victoria was gathering purplestem asters beside her when Wyatt took her into his arms.

His lips were luscious.

She yearned to have more of him, all of him.

But that would not do.

"We best head back for dinner," she whispered, stroking his cheek.

Was this love?

*   *   *

Their time together was not all nonchalance and leisure, kisses and caresses. Wyatt was serious, always thinking. Victoria loved that.

And Wyatt had plans. "Insurance company. As most white firms will not take our business, I say carpe diem! Turn an obstacle into an opportunity. I aim to create something more efficient than a mutual aid society."

Victoria's heart went into double beats when Wyatt said that he planned to open his first office in Washington.

"Why not New York City?" she asked.

"North of the Mason-Dixon, Washington has the largest colored population and more colored people of means than any other city. Besides, my uncle has more connections here than I have in New York. I will need investors." Victoria learned that Wyatt had definitely been doing his homework. A voracious reader like her, he had been gobbling up book after book on Washington.

"When I am done with this I will pass it on to you," he said one evening as they sat in the Proctor's sitting room. She was reading *The Portrait of a Lady*. He *The Gilded Age*.

"What is it about?"

"The national capital. It was published some years back, but I am told that it captures Washington to a tee and that when it comes to corruptions and other shenanigans, the city has not changed much since Twain and a friend wrote the book."

"Mark Twain?"

"None other."

"Then it must be wickedly funny."

Wyatt smiled broadly. "It is."

Wyatt was strong, bold, had a mind of his own. He seemed able to tackle any subject.

From the death of Jesse James—"No honor among thieves," he remarked.

To the hanging of Garfield's assassin—"I could never support the death penalty, especially when someone is clearly insane."

And there was the more recent death of Mary Todd Lincoln, and Thomas Edison's Pearl Street Power Station— "I have read that this power station will provide electricity to a square mile of homes and businesses in lower Manhattan."

"Do you think this electricity will really work? I've not read that much about it, but it sounds so strange. Light without fire?"

"I think it will work. I think electricity will be part of our future."

Wyatt had already told her that he would only be gone about a month. "If I can wrap things up any sooner, I surely will."

"You promise?" she had asked with a winsome smile just before she pulled back her bowstring and let fly an arrow.

Bull's-eye.

"I promise."

Calm and collected when speaking on most subjects, Wyatt became very worked up about the new immigration laws. "After how many Chinese men—hundreds—died building the transcontinental railroad, now they ban them from entering the country." Wyatt frowned. "Sign of the times if you ask me."

"What do you mean?"

"Have you read about the lawsuits people have brought over accommodations? There is one against the Memphis and Charleston Railroad—"

"Oh, yes, the Robinsons."

"And in New York against the Grand Opera House."

"As I recall there are a few more cases of challenges to the color line being drawn."

"Trying to make whites abide by the Civil Rights Act."

"That was when?"

Wyatt rubbed his chin. "1876. No, 1875."

"Pray God they succeed."

"I hope so but I am not that confident. There is something in the wind. I think we need to brace ourselves. True, we have a handful of lawsuits against discrimination, but I have heard of a boatload of instances of colored denied a hotel room, made to ride in a baggage car, barred from an orchestra seat, instances that did not result in a lawsuit. People simply swallowed the insult.

"I have been told that here in the last year several dining saloons have stopped allowing us in," said Victoria. "Unless it is someone like Frederick Douglass."

"Perhaps the day will come when Washington will no longer be the colored man's paradise."

They were seated on the steps leading down to the spring with its bright green reeds and small boulders. They watched as the water bubbled and eddied.

Victoria sighed. "We have produced a Frederick Douglass, a Daniel Murray, an Orindatus Simon Bolívar Wall, not to mention your uncle. And in your New York City there is the caterer Peter Downing, whose brother George has that fine hotel in Newport. I read somewhere that they are worth about $250,000."

"Your point?"

"There is ample evidence that if given half a chance so many of our people can amount to something, rise, contribute to society. It is so galling!"

"Until more of them get right with God we will always have to be twice as good to get half as far." Wyatt brightened. "But then we do have a talent for making a way out of no way."

Though a realist, Wyatt was such an optimist, always walked in the light. And there was his absolute lack of appetite for gossip! He never had an unkind word to say about anyone.

And honesty. Wyatt was so committed to honesty. Victoria learned that the day before he left for New York.

"I want you to know that I am not here by happenstance," he said as they took tea on the Proctor's back veranda.

Victoria returned her potted salmon and watercress sandwich to its plate. "What do you mean?"

"I came here on purpose. For you."

"For me?"

"A few weeks back I saw you at the Fitzhughs' soiree."

"Were we introduced?" Again Victoria feigned ignorance.

"No, but the minute I saw you . . . well, I continued to observe you."

Victoria had a hard time looking Wyatt in the eye. She reached for her cup of tea.

"I knew instantly that I wanted to get to know you. So I made some inquiries. When I learned that you had gone to Proctor's Resort I lost no time in booking a room."

"Wyatt, you are certainly—"

"Certainly what?"

"I do not know—"

"I am merely being aboveboard, thought it best to be honest. Just as I aim to run an honest business I have always run an honest life. So I wanted you to know that I sought you out. Know, too, that when I mean to do business, I do business."

"Oh, now I am business, Wyatt?" she teased.

He tapped her nose. "Yes, Victoria. My heart's only business."

ALL MY GOOD COLOR?

The month seemed a year.

Easing the ache was a telegram every few days.

"THINKING OF YOU—TOO MUCH!" ... "THE WRAPPING UP IS GOING QUICKLY. CANNOT WAIT."

Victoria lost no time in replying.

"DREAMED THAT WE WERE AT PROCTOR'S RESORT. SKETCHED THE SPRING." ... "HURRY!"

The night before Wyatt's return, Victoria was a wreck.

She worked herself into a near panic imagining the train running off the track. Of Wyatt's affections cooling, of—

What should she wear?

The simple white poplin with high lace collar?

The cream organza dotted with bouquets of violets?

She tried on several outfits before finally settling on the bright-rose silk walking dress with rows of lace up the front. If they did indeed decide to go for a walk, she would top it off with her white chip hat trimmed with Spanish lace, pink-velvet ribbon, and a modest pink feather.

Oddly enough, Victoria slept very well that night.

The following day was a slow drip. Victoria did her level best to busy herself. Reading. Needlework. Sketching. Reading.

By three o'clock in the afternoon she was glued to a bedroom window seat.

Waiting.

As a stream of boys on velocipedes sped by.

As a tall, stern-looking man wearing a bowler hat a bit small for his head tapped his cane on the pavement every other step.

As a Western Union messenger knocked on a door across the street.

Waiting.

Waiting.

Waiting.

Thinking about how far she had come. Truly a world away from Forest City. If only Ma Clara—

Never look back! It is excessively ill-bred.

Waiting.

When the sun went shy, it took her back to her early days in Baltimore when she felt so lonely, when—

Never look back! It is excessively ill-bred.

Waiting.

Then not waiting.

Victoria jumped up at the sight of Wyatt turning the corner. She rushed from her room, caught herself at the landing. Quickly she returned to her window seat. She picked up a book along the way.

Waiting.

For the doorbell to ring.

She opened the book.

Waiting.

For Mrs. Rodgers to answer the door.

Waiting.

For his voice, for the sound of the door closing, for the footsteps, for Mrs. Rodgers's rap on her door.

"Yes?"

"Missy, a Mr. Riddle has come to call."

"Thank you, Mrs. Rodgers." Victoria mustered up all the reserve she could. "Please tell him that I will be down momentarily."

Deep, slow breaths.

Deep, slow breaths.

Deep, slow breaths.

She checked her face in the mirror. Confident that she looked sufficiently serene, Victoria headed down to the sitting room.

* * *

"My dear Wyatt!"

He was on his feet. Soon by her side, kissing her cheeks, then her hand.

If only she could wrap her arms around him. If only he could scoop her up and twirl her around the room.

But that would not do.

Mrs. Rodgers brought in refreshments. An hour later Dorcas Vashon came down. She invited Wyatt to stay for dinner.

Victoria and Wyatt were inseparable, with their long, languid walks around the city, with their favorite picnic spot in Lincoln Park, a spot not far from the monument to Emancipation.

Penelope Fitzhugh did not approve. "Victoria, is it really serious?" she asked one day during a game of hearts.

"Why, whatever do you mean?"

"Do not play coy with me. You know very well that I am speaking of Wyatt Riddle. You really must not—"

"I must not what?"

"You cannot seriously be contemplating, you know . . ."

"What would be so wrong with that?"

"He has no real money, and this business scheme of his is dubious."

Fanny Miller also disapproved. "And think, my dear girl, if you marry him all your good color will go to waste!"

"All my good color?"

"The children you would have with him. They would most certainly be brown, perhaps as black as him."

In a short story or novel, Victoria had read of a character livid to the point of wanting to throttle another character. She had wondered what that much rage felt like.

Now she knew.

A few days later Victoria was in a panic over something that had absolutely nothing to do with mean ole Fanny Miller and Penelope Fitzhugh.

THE PEOPLE WHO KNEW
ME BEST

"And how may I help you?" asked perky Bella.

"I somehow managed to lose one of my kid gloves," the young woman replied.

Victoria was in Miss Dahlia's small shop trying on a steel-gray bonnet with ombré feathers when the girl in need of gloves stepped inside.

Victoria had come for a combination corset, petticoat, and bustle. It was easier on the spine, she had read, chuckling when she saw that the undergarment was actually called "the Victoria." She forgot all about the Victoria when the bonnet caught her eye. A matching Medici collarette was on the mannequin beside it.

Victoria had not turned around when the bell above the shop door did its *ting-a-ling*, but after she heard the young woman speak she froze.

There was no mistaking the accent. There was something familiar about the voice.

Victoria removed the bonnet and hurriedly reached for her black felt top hat with dotted swiss lace veil that fell to her nose. She headed for the door.

"Oh, Miss Victoria!" the shop girl called out.

Victoria stopped. "Yes?"

"The shawls your aunt ordered have come in. I'll get them for you now."

"No need, Bella. I can come back another time, as you are waiting on someone." Victoria had yet to turn around.

"Do you mind?" Bella asked the young woman at the counter.

"Not at all" was her reply.

"Really there is no—"

"I'll have them wrapped and ready in a jiffy."

Silly goose. How could you let yourself get so spooked by a voice?

She headed for the counter.

Lost-glove girl looked up at her and smiled.

Victoria responded with a very forced smile.

It was worse than she had feared. She could never forget that chestnut face, those wide-set, witching eyes with their hooded lids. She looked down and saw a heart-shaped birthmark on the back of the young woman's right hand.

What is she doing in Washington?

"That's awfully lovely," said Sarah Pace, admiring Victoria's terra-cotta *visite* trimmed in gold fringe.

"Thank you."

"I've never seen anything like that back home."

"And where might that be?" asked Bella.

Victoria was beside herself with fear. *Bella, please, just get on with wrapping!* she wanted to scream.

"Savannah," replied Sarah Pace.

"Oh, and what brings you to Washington?"

Bella, please!

"Oh, I'm just passing through with my aunt Drusilla. We are on our way to Philadelphia. We thought it would be nice to visit the capital for a few days. Our train leaves later today."

"Here you go, Miss Victoria."

As soon as Bella placed the package into her hands, Victoria gave her a clipped thank-you and headed for the door. She managed a quick "Good day to you both" before she reached it. As she opened the door, she hesitated. The *ting-a-ling* seemed extremely loud.

She swallowed, took a deep breath, sailed through the door.

What if Sarah Pace had recognized me? Let it out right there in the shop who I really am?

Bella was a gossip. Before dinnertime the news would have been all over town.

"You look as if you have seen a ghost," said Dorcas Vashon when she passed Victoria in the hallway.

"Oh, just a little weary." She headed up to her room cloaked in dread.

What if there is a problem with their train? What if Sarah Pace and her aunt Drusilla do not leave today?

Victoria did not dare leave the house for days. With invitations she had accepted she sent her regrets. When Wyatt suggested a stroll, she suggested they play cards or checkers or chess in the sitting room.

"You do no quite seem yourself," he said one evening.

Just then Victoria realized she had missed out on a chance to capture one of Wyatt's rooks. "I am fine. Just a bit of a headache."

What if Wyatt ever finds out?

"How many other people who know me from Savannah might come here?"

Victoria and Dorcas Vashon were in the backyard, where the older woman pruned roses while the younger tended to the herb garden she had planted in a pocket of the yard months back. Victoria had bordered her garden with oyster shells.

Several days had passed since that close encounter with Sarah Pace, and Victoria was just now telling Dorcas Vashon about it.

"But, my dear, think about this simple fact: this Sarah Pace did not recognize you."

"But what if——"

"Victoria, do not borrow trouble."

Victoria felt somewhat comforted, then a tinge sad. "And what are the chances that Ma Clara, Miss Abby, or Binah will ever come to the capital?"

"Precisely."

"Or ferryman Jack." Victoria saw herself singing "Free-willum" all those years ago.

"Who?"

"Just a man who used to ferry me over to Shad Island . . . The people who knew me best, they would recognize me, but probably no one else from Savannah." Victoria thought of Old Man Boney too.

The people who knew me best.

There had been that moment of hesitation in Miss Dahlia's shop, that split second when she had an urge to reveal herself to Sarah Pace and ask her about the people who knew her best despite the fact that deep down she knew that Sarah Pace would not give Ma Clara, Binah, and Miss Abby the time of day, let alone keep up with their lives.

Onward! Victoria had told herself. *Onward!*

BAY RUM

Victoria was not due back for a few more hours, but shortly after she and Claire met at Miss Carrie's Tea Room, Claire came down with a dreadful headache.

Victoria had walked her home and then headed for the house with the mansard roof, intending to change into something more suitable for sketching out back.

When Victoria entered the house she was brought up short by the sight of a man's lightweight frock coat hanging on the coat rack.

Wyatt had a coat like that.

Victoria stepped closer, allowed herself a sniff. Bay rum.

Wyatt's scent.

Why are the sitting room's sliding doors closed?

Victoria tiptoed over, put an ear to the door.

Voices.

Wyatt's.

Dorcas Vashon's.

Victoria tiptoed to the kitchen in search of Mrs. Rodgers.

With the back door ajar, she saw Mrs. Rodgers hanging laundry on the line.

"Mrs. Rodgers, is that Mr. Riddle in the sitting room with my aunt?"

"Yes, Missy."

Odd. He knew that I was seeing Claire today.

"When did he arrive?"

"About an hour ago," replied Mrs. Rodgers with two clothespins between her teeth.

"He came calling for me?"

"No, Missy, for Miss Dorcas."

Puzzled, Victoria headed up to her room. To wait.

Her heart skipped a beat when she heard the sitting room doors slide open.

Footsteps headed for the front door.

The front door closed.

Victoria tipped over to a window, saw Wyatt walking away, hands in his pockets, striding easy.

She did everything in her power not to fly down the steps.

Perhaps he had come to speak with Dorcas Vashon about investing in his insurance business.

Or perhaps—

Someone was coming up the stairs.

There was a knock on her door. "Missy?"

"Yes, Mrs. Rodgers?"

"Your aunt would like you to join her in the sitting room."

Victoria could not read Dorcas Vashon's face. A strange look.

Serious yet pleased.

"How was your tea?"

"Tea ended before it began. Claire came down with a wicked headache."

"I see." Dorcas Vashon tapped her fingers on the armchair.

Silence.

"Has something happened?" Victoria was trying hard not to worry.

"Not yet, my dear, but I do have some news. Your Mr. Riddle has asked for your hand." Dorcas Vashon was smiling.

Victoria went weak in the knees. She headed for a chair. "He wants to—"

"He most certainly does."

"What did you say?"

Silence.

"I told him that while I appreciated the courtesy, marriage was entirely your decision."

Silence.

"It is?"

"Yes, my dear, it is."

"Well, what do you think?" Victoria tried not to wring her hands.

"I think that he is a fine young man. Has pluck. And it is very clear to me that he absolutely adores you. But in the end, my dear, you must harken to your heart. That is, while at the same time, you keep your wits about you."

For the rest of the day Victoria floated. Floated back up to her room, where she stared at herself in the mirror. Floated while changing her clothes. Floated through Mrs. Rodgers's dinner for her of mulligatawny soup, venison chops, mashed potatoes, and green peas. For Dorcas Vashon, added to the mashed potatoes and the peas, there was corn and stewed tomatoes.

That night Victoria fell asleep with *The Ladies' Book of Etiquette* in her hands. She had decided to reread chapter twenty-three: "On a Young Lady's Conduct When Contemplating Marriage."

BENEATH A HARVEST MOON

A simple band of gold. In the center, a round cut emerald encircled by rose cut diamonds.

When Victoria said yes, she longed to be even more of a lady, yearned to do all that she could to make Wyatt happy. She would host however many luncheons and dinners for clients and prospective clients and investors. She would attend a million functions if that's what he needed her to do. She would do her utmost to help him build his business. Then, in the midst of daydreams, conscience called.

Should she tell him?

Was it right to enter into marriage with a lie?

Keeping her secret from others had never bothered her. But Wyatt was not others. She had been tempted to tell him the truth on more than one occasion, especially after running into Sarah Pace.

*　*　*

He stayed for dinner after he went on bended knee in the sitting room. Victoria was too giddy to eat much, but she savored the way he enjoyed himself. The way he so masterfully carved the roast chicken, how he allowed himself a second helping of scalloped potatoes. And Dorcas Vashon was all smiles over her salad and tomato soup.

There was a nip in the night when Victoria saw Wyatt to the door. And they kissed beneath a harvest moon.

Wyatt pulled back, took her hands in his. "Someone across the street might be looking out a window."

"Let them," said Victoria. She pulled Wyatt to her. "One more."

Later, up in her bedroom, in a window seat, gazing at the moon, Victoria imagined the hugs from the folks back home if they knew that she was to marry someone as wonderful as Wyatt. The thought of Ma Clara not being a witness to the wedding brought tears to Victoria's eyes.

And dear Wyatt…

Tell him or not to tell him?

She longed for a sign.

A shooting star.

A sudden gust of wind.

Something.

Never look back! It is excessively ill-bred.

But was it right to go forward without going back?

TOO GOOD A PERSON TO
DECEIVE

The plan had been for Wyatt to come to dinner on Saturday, but Victoria made a change.

Before Mrs. Rodgers went marketing on Thursday morning, Victoria handed the woman her own list of groceries and bade her to deliver a note for Wyatt to the Motts' home.

Picnic instead on Saturday?
V.

When Mrs. Rodgers returned from shopping she had his reply.

Marvelous.
W.

At their favorite picnic spot under blue-sky blue, after Wyatt laid out the blankets, Victoria laid out the food.

Cold salmon with hollandaise sauce.

Cold ham with French mustard.

Cucumber sandwiches.

Lobster salad.

Potato salad.

Asparagus and cauliflower salad with a light lemon dressing.

Squab pie.

A fruit tart.

Pickles, jellies, relishes, bread, creamed butter.

"You are too good to me!" Wyatt exclaimed when Victoria brought out the deviled eggs. "You don't even like them."

"But you do and so it was my pleasure to make you a batch."

"You? Not Mrs. Rodgers?"

"I even made the lemonade."

Three little girls filed by playing hoop and stick.

Nearby a couple laughed out loud.

Somewhere in the distance a baby bawled, whisking Victoria into a daydream of her and Wyatt in this same spot one day, her with a baby in her arms.

All your good color will go to waste!

Let it! Victoria wanted nothing more than to cradle brown babies, babies with no trace of the father she never knew, babies she would lavish with love. Most of all she hoped for at least one daughter, so she could give her everything she never had, a proper mother-daughter bond. She would pay close attention to her children *all the time*.

Wyatt interrupted her daydream with some news.

"I think I may have found our home."

A bit of wind picked up.

"Oh, really?"

"Pending your approval, of course."

"Well, where is it?"

"M Street. 900 block. We can start the business in the basement."

Victoria knew that block. "Claire lives on that block. When can I see it?"

"How about on Monday?"

All Victoria could think about was how wonderful Wyatt was. Too good a person to deceive.

She took a sip of lemonade.

"Wyatt, there is something I need to discuss—to tell you."

LONG WALK HOME

He looked appalled, horrified. His silence was a slap.

Confounded, confused, Victoria held up the plate of deviled eggs. "Would you care for another?"

Wyatt winced. "You sound so nonchalant," he snapped. "What would make you think that I could possibly want to eat *anything* after what you have just told me." He turned his back on Victoria, drew his knees to his chest.

Victoria, raised plate still in her hand, was paralyzed. Finally she lowered the plate.

Hands trembling.

Mouth quivering.

A dam about to burst.

"I thought the—thought you would appreciate honesty, I thought—"

"Who else knows?" he asked.

At that moment Victoria was glad that he had turned

his back on her. His voice was so steely. She imagined his scowl. "Only Dorcas Vashon and Miss Hardwick, who is not even in Washington."

"What about Mr. and Mrs. Rodgers?"

"No. I do not think so. I do not know." She fought back tears. "Wyatt, please . . . I only meant to—would you have preferred that I—"

"It is a lot to take in, Victoria, or whatever your name is. It is as if I don't even know you."

"You *do* know me, Wyatt. I am the same person you first saw at the Fitzhughs' soiree, the same person you sought out at Proctor's Resort. No different." She tapped her chest. "This is me. This is who I am now."

Wyatt hung his head. "How could I ever trust you?"

A beautiful life was vanishing before her eyes. "I swear to you I will *never* tell another living soul."

"I don't mean trust you to keep your dirty little secret. I mean trust you with . . . about anything."

Your ma is a—

"No one else will *ever* know."

"*I* know!" he spat. "For goodness' sake, have you no shame?"

There it was again. The thing that had hounded her all her life.

Your ma is a—

"Shame? No, Wyatt, I am not ashamed of what I have done. I did nothing *wrong*. I simply said yes to an opportunity of a lifetime. If only you truly understood how hard I worked. If only you really knew the hell pit I grew up in! If only you truly understood how I fought to not end up like my mother . . . How can you not be proud of me in light of how far I have come. Before Miss Hardwick I knew nothing of fish forks and such, of etiquette. Those months of training were grueling. At one point I thought I would break and I ran away, but I went *back*, more determined than ever to do *whatever* it took to rise in life. I *persevered*. How, Wyatt, how on earth can you speak of shame?"

Victoria inched over, put a hand on his shoulder.

When he recoiled she burst into tears.

"Please don't make a scene!"

Victoria moved away, clamped a hand over her mouth. Harnessing every bit of reserve she could, she dried her eyes, began to pack the picnic basket. Silence seemed the best, the only course. There was nothing that she could say, do.

Never look back!

She rebuked herself for not hewing to that advice.

Not her soft hands, not her poise, not her ability to set a table for a three- or seven-course meal. None of it mattered. Not today. Not ever.

Wyatt stood up, began to pace, rub his chin. The anger seemed to have subsided.

A bit.

Victoria could only hope—

"In Savannah, when you lived in your mother's house were you . . ."

Victoria's pain shifted to rage as she realized what was really on Wyatt's mind, what he was fishing for. *How dare he!*

"Wyatt, ask your question."

Silence.

Wyatt stopped pacing, hung his head. "I am just trying to get the full picture."

The golden leaves blanketing the grass. The red, orange, and lingering green leaves on maples and other trees. The sunshine and clear blue sky. Everything that made this Indian summer day so wondrous now seemed to mock Victoria.

She thought for a moment. Should she remain silent, make him ask the question, let those words come out of his mouth? Or should she put his mind to rest? *What difference will it make?* she concluded.

Wyatt barely looked at her, then once again turned his back on her. He ran a hand over his head down the back of his neck, massaged it. He shoved his hands into his pockets. "I feel bewitched," he said, looking absolutely lost.

Victoria frowned. "Bewitched? What are you talking about?"

"It's, it's like you put a spell on me. I saw you for the first time at that soiree. With no introduction, without a single conversation between us there I was trying to find out about you, find out where you went when you left the city." Wyatt turned around again. This time he craned his neck and stared up at the sky.

That baby began bawling again.

"It's just not like me. It was impulsive. Too quick. I should have done more fact-finding before I . . ."

Victoria, too distressed, destroyed to say another word, finished packing the picnic basket. When done she rose, removed the basket from atop the blankets.

Wyatt shook out the blankets, folded them up, stowed them in the hamper by his feet.

Their eyes met briefly.

Victoria made sure the picnic basket's lock was secure as Wyatt reached for the blanket hamper.

In Savannah, when you lived in your mother's house were you—

"Wyatt?"

"Yes."

Victoria looked down, slipped the emerald-and-diamond ring from her finger. "I imagine that you would like to have this back."

Wyatt put the blanket hamper down, took the ring from her trembling hand, swiftly tucked it into his waistcoat pocket.

It was a long walk home.

NEVER LOOK BACK!

Victoria entered that house with the mansard roof as quietly as she could. Relieved not to see Dorcas Vashon in either the sitting room or the parlor, she tiptoed down to the kitchen, placed the picnic basket on the counter, dropped the blanket hamper on the floor.

She tensed at the sound of footsteps up above, on the landing, coming down the stairs, then stopping at the door that led down to the kitchen.

Best to make herself busy. She began putting things away. Leftover food in the icebox, dishes and cutlery in the sink.

"Is that you, Victoria?"

"Yes, Aunt Dorcas."

Please don't let her come down here.

Her eyes were still red-rimmed and swollen.

"I did not expect you back so early," said Dorcas Vashon.

"I began to feel unwell."

"How unwell?" Dorcas Vashon took a step down. "Shall I—"

"It's not serious. More like I'm just tired."

"Where is Wyatt?"

"At the Motts' by now I expect."

"Hmm," said Dorcas Vashon, then she returned to the hallway.

When Victoria could tell that she had gone into the sitting room, she hurried up to her bedroom.

When no more tears would flow, Victoria rose from her bed, washed her face. She curled up into a window seat, stared at a now-stony sky. Every so often she went to her dressing table mirror to see what shape her eyes were in. Not until they were no longer red-rimmed and swollen did she venture downstairs. She was only there long enough to find Mrs. Rodgers.

She was out back picking herbs.

"Mrs. Rodgers, for dinner I would just like to have some broth."

"Yes, Missy."

"Up in my room, please."

"Yes, Missy."

Victoria again feigned sickness the following day, fretting about what to do next. If she kept claiming to be sick Dorcas Vashon would bring in a doctor.

But Victoria was terrified at the thought of leaving the house. Not to church. Not to anything. Not anywhere where she might run into Wyatt.

As she paced, she panicked.

What has Wyatt told his family?

Will he broadcast the truth about me?

What will this mean for Dorcas Vashon?

"I should have spoken to her," Victoria muttered. Just when she thought she had a handle on life she had gone and made a foolish, foolish mistake. The greatest blunder of her life. She had shattered her own dream.

Up in her room, in her solitude Victoria sketched. The street below. Wormley's. Lafayette Square. Then she went back.

To that narrow house in Baltimore with first-floor shutters askew.

To the tubby man in the brown sack coat and brown pants and wearing a broad-brimmed hat. Walking briskly.

That boy with a cart of melons.

The wide woman scrubbing steps.

The scary clock from which a monk popped out.

Miss Doone.

Miss Graves.

Then Victoria went back to Forest City.

Never look back!

What difference does it make now?

Back to the ragtag warehouses and offices that made up Factors Row.

Green Mansion.

Miss Abby's boardinghouse.

She made Ma Clara's eyes larger than they actually were, never quite able to capture their twinkle.

In a portrait of Binah, Victoria dispensed with the spectacles, made both her arms the same length.

In a sketch of Old Man Boney she added canopies to his oxcarts as she wondered what his given name was. She figured "Boney" must be his real last name. After all, he was quite plump.

Humming "Freewillum," Victoria sketched ferryman Jack.

Victoria put her drawing sticks and sketch pad down, walked over to her dresser. From the back of the top drawer she brought out a pouch containing those coral beads. She'd ask Mrs. Rodgers to take them to a jeweler to be restrung when next she had an errand to run.

Just then there was a knock on her bedroom door.

"Yes?"

"May I come in?"

"Yes."

RAISED AN EYEBROW

When Dorcas Vashon entered, Victoria saw her eye the coral beads. She expected her to inquire about them.

Dorcas Vashon didn't. Instead, with her right hand clasped around her left wrist, she asked, "My dear, would you like to tell me what is going on?"

Victoria swallowed, flailed around inside for a lie. "The engagement is off," she finally replied.

Dorcas Vashon raised an eyebrow. "My dear, what happened?"

"We just decided that we are not truly suited for each other."

"You are lying, my dear."

After a long, painful silence, Victoria proceeded to tell Dorcas Vashon what happened during that picnic in the park.

LIKE LEAD INTO THE SEA

"I'm sorry. I didn't think," said Victoria, head hung and too afraid to look Dorcas Vashon in the eye.

"Think what?"

"Think of speaking with you about it beforehand."

Dorcas Vashon patted her back.

"In telling him about me I told him about you."

"What exactly did you tell him about me?"

"Only that you are a wealthy woman from Charleston who took pity on me during a visit to Savannah and that you offered me a better life, that you go around eager to help people of promise rise in life."

Dorcas Vashon took Victoria by the shoulders. "Look at me, my dear."

Slowly Victoria raised her head.

"Now tell me, do you think Wyatt will let others know what you told him?"

One moment Victoria was shaking her head, the next on the verge of tears. "I honestly don't know. I just don't know. I'm so sorry. I'm so ashamed."

"Victoria, how many times must I tell you: there is no place for shame in your life."

Spent, Victoria now had no compunction about asking Dorcas Vashon something she had long wanted to know. "Did you know about my mother?"

Dorcas Vashon nodded. "I made inquiries after I first glimpsed your potential. I found you all the more remarkable after I learned of your beginnings." Dorcas Vashon stepped over to the window, looked out. "Now back to Wyatt. You may have made a mistake, and most mistakes can be remedied . . . Or you may have been wiser than you realized."

"What do you mean?"

"Well, in telling Wyatt the truth, you tested him."

"But—I gave back the ring and he took it."

"Did he hesitate?"

Victoria thought back, saw him put the blanket hamper down, then in one smooth move take the ring from her hand and put it into his waistcoat pocket.

"No, there was no hesitation."

"It sounds as if shock was the ruling emotion."

"What are you saying?"

"From what I have observed of Wyatt he likes order. What you told him, well, it disordered him. Shock passes."

After a pause Dorcas Vashon added, "If, indeed, Wyatt finds shame where there is none, well then, he is not the man for you."

Was there really hope? "What should I do now?"

"Have patience. And in the meantime we will say that you have gone to Baltimore to visit relatives."

Hope was hard. No amount of finery, no amount of polite conversation, no amount of poise and proper gait could change the fact that she was the daughter of a—

Where once she had dreamed of being an asset to Wyatt, she knew now that she would only be a liability. "The Rime of the Ancient Mariner" came to mind.

> *And from my neck so free*
> *The Albatross fell off, and sank*
> *Like lead into the sea.*

But maybe Dorcas Vashon was right. If he found shame . . .

Victoria took most of her meals in her room. When she set the tray on the floor outside, the food was half-eaten.

She paced, tried not to think.

When she took up a book, it was a hazy read.

When she looked out the window, the people, the sky—everything seemed dull, faded.

Finally, with a drawing stick and sketch pad Victoria went back again to Forest City.

To Strangers' Ground. In a flight of fancy she rendered Spanish moss as big thick braids.

To that saltbox house on Minis Street. From the front on a sun-drenched day. At eventide too. Under moonlight with frightened eyes peering out from the attic window.

And then there was a face she had never, ever thought of sketching.

Pouty mouth.

Doe eyes sad and full of pain.

In slavery her whitefolks abused her every which way, left her broken in mind. Because of things they made her do, your ma came to believe she had no talent for nothing except, well...

The irony struck her. She had so hoped that Wyatt would understand, yet she had never tried to understand Mamma. Only judged, faulted, despised. What exactly her ma endured, she would never know. Just as she would never know why Mamma had held on to those coral beads and hadn't done up her room in red.

Maybe Mamma did the best that she could. Maybe had she had a Ma Clara... Maybe if she had had a Dorcas Vashon...

Tears that failed to flow more than a year ago when she

stood in Strangers' Ground beneath that brooding, wind-swept sky . . .

Victoria wept to the point of trembling, sketch pad and drawing stick fallen to the floor.

"I'm so sorry, Mamma!" she sobbed. "Sorry for the way we parted . . . Sorry I stopped praying for you . . . Sorry for not rushing to your side when Ma Clara told me you had the waste-away. Dear God, forgive me!"

Victoria's appetite had returned by the time she sat down with Dorcas Vashon for the autumn feast. Cream of mush-room soup. Oyster pie. Chestnut stuffing. There were also mashed turnips, baked sweet potatoes, winter squash, suc-cotash, and jellied cranberry sauce. Victoria had suggested roast pheasant over turkey or squab. For dessert there was pumpkin pie.

Carving the bird, Victoria thought hard about the mean-ing of the day. Yes, she had lost Wyatt, but she still had so much to be grateful for. A beautiful place to live. Splendid clothes. For breakfast she never had to make do with pick-les or a stale biscuit.

Not things to take lightly.

She thought about the Bay Street orphans, young Binah, young her. Maybe she would ask Dorcas Vashon to invest in that little school and home she once dreamed of. Then Victoria thought better. *The alley dwellers. That is what I will do. I will start a club to aid the alley dwellers.*

She would visit with mothers, teach them things about nutrition and hygiene. She would raise money for food, clothing, home repairs, doctors' visits. She wondered how many of the children went to school. "Mothers' Helpers," that's what she would call it.

If Dorcas Vashon decided that it was best to leave the capital, then she would start her Mothers' Helpers club in the new city. There was sure to be colored in need of a helping hand no matter where they went.

That night Victoria also decided that she was done with hiding, with feeling defeated. Once again she made up her mind to persevere. The day after Thanksgiving she picked up from her desk an envelope that had arrived a few days earlier.

*Mrs. Fitzhugh requests the pleasure of
Miss Victoria Vashon's company,
on Saturday, December 23rd at 8 o'clock
to take part in a Christmas Gala.*

Victoria reached for notepaper and a pen.

*Miss Victoria Vashon accepts with
pleasure Mrs. Fitzhugh's polite invitation
to the Christmas Gala.*

FULL OF CHRISTMAS CHEER

The Fitzhugh double parlor was clear of much of its furniture.

Side chairs ringed the rooms with rectangular tables, round tables, and in the center of the larger room an octagon.

All covered with mint-green tablecloths.

All heavy-laden with food, from elaborate pyramids of fruit to silver trays of cheeses and roast beef along with crystal dishes of Oysters à la Poulette, spiced oysters, fried oysters, and platters of tea sandwiches.

On one round table sat a large crystal bowl of eggnog encircled by gleaming crystal punch cups.

In corners stood tall sentinels of shining silver planters offering up stems of holly and cranberry branches, tufts of pine. The arches, doorways, like the mantels, were draped in luscious green garlands. The Fitzhughs had really gone all out.

Victoria saw more than a few heads turn when she stepped into the room in one of Madame Keckley's creations: a flowing emerald taffeta gown with a square neckline, square collar, fitted bodice, and long frill-ringed bell-shaped sleeves. At first Victoria had resisted the large bow on either side of the bustline.

"It is not too much?" Victoria had asked.

"No at all," replied Madame Keckley. "With your height you can pull it off." Then the modiste continued reviewing her sketch. "The bows will join vertical rows of frills that will run under the arm, then up over the shoulder and around the back of the neck. Your skirt, gathered tightly at the waist, will feature ruffle-trimmed crescent-shaped panels to join a simple bustle in the back."

I could probably pull off two bows! Victoria thought as she stood in the Fitzhugh parlor. Once again she felt like a Cinderella. She had decided against earbobs, a bracelet, and such. The only jewelry she wore was around her neck: those restrung coral beads.

With her best party smile on, Victoria tried to read people's eyes. She looked for traces of disgust or pity. She saw none. Pleased, she was also puzzled.

"Beautiful Victoria, so glad you could come!" said Mrs. Fitzhugh, pulling Victoria farther into the room.

"I am ever so grateful for the invitation," said Victoria sweetly.

"And here you are, lovely Victoria!" Timothy Fitzhugh rushed over with a cup of eggnog.

Victoria was soon besieged.

"Victoria, so good to see you!"

"Victoria, when did you return?"

"Victoria, how was Baltimore?"

"Victoria, you'll never guess what happened while you were away!"

She began to breathe easier. Had Wyatt told others her secret, there would have been snide remarks, some rolling of the eyes. Too, had he broadcast that they had broken off the engagement surely someone would have let drop a comment such as "What a shame about you and Wyatt."

Perhaps, though, Wyatt told only his family and asked them to keep mum for the time being.

Utterly at ease, before long Victoria was laughing, chit-chatting, exchanging pleasantries.

And fanning herself in the packed parlor.

Am I coming down with something? She excused herself. "I simply must get some air." She headed for the sitting room across the hall to get her cloak, then for the front door. When she opened it—

"Well, hello there."

Victoria almost jumped out of her skin. Speechless, she just stared at him.

Gray-striped pants. Black Prince Albert frock coat. Silver-gray jacquard waistcoat. His white shirt had a high-stand wing-tip collar. His white cravat was tied in a cascade. On his feet, patent leather Congress gaiters. His silk top hat was in his hand.

He looked magnificent.

She noticed the sharpness of his mustache and hairline. He must have been in a barber's chair that morning.

"Hello," Victoria finally said. A whisper.

"I heard that you had accepted."

"Indeed." She looked past his shoulder, trying to get unflustered.

"Are you leaving?"

"No. I just need a bit of air."

He offered his arm.

"Hadn't you better go inside and pay your respects to our hosts?"

"That can wait."

He offered his arm again.

Victoria took it. Head held high, she walked with Wyatt down the steps.

"Hello, Victoria! Hello, Wyatt!" shouted new arrivals full of Christmas cheer.

They both waved, neither speaking until they reached the end of the long walkway.

"You look lovely."

"Thank you."

"How have you been?"

"Fine."

"I was told that you went to Baltimore."

What difference did it make if she let him know of another lie. "That's what was said, as I wanted to avoid society. I have been here all the time."

A strange look came over Wyatt's face. She decided to nip things in the bud. "Yes, Wyatt, it was a lie, another lie."

"No, no, I did not mean—I understand why you, why you . . ."

She had never seen him at a loss for words.

"I have not been much in society either. I have been putting all my energy into the business—reading actuary books and thinking about potential clients, mostly."

Victoria looked at the wreaths at the windows of the Fitzhugh home, at the window boxes overflowing with pine cuttings cradling gold ornaments. She wondered if there would be snow. Inside they were singing Christmas carols.

Finally Victoria looked in his direction. "Wyatt?"

"Yes."

"I would like to know, so that I can prepare myself, so that Dorcas Vashon can prepare herself too . . ." She looked him in the eye. "While I know I can have no expectations of you, as a last courtesy I would like to know when you told your family that we broke off the engagement, what reason did you give?"

Wyatt fidgeted with his top hat. "None."

"What do you mean, none?"

"I have not said anything to anyone."

"Well, when you do tell them, what will you say?"

Wyatt put his top hat on his head. "Do me a favor, Victoria, go back inside and tell the Fitzhughs that you are feeling unwell. Then I can walk you home and we can talk."

"Feeling unwell? Lie? You want me to lie, Wyatt? *You?*"

"Touché." His smile didn't mask the sadness in his eyes.

Victoria looked away. To steady herself she thought about how heartless he had been.

Your dirty little secret.

Have you no shame?

She willed herself a heart of stone. She would not be moved.

"Wyatt, I can understand that you were shocked. But you were so cruel."

"I know. I'm sorry. So sorry!"

"And that question you started to ask."

"What question?"

"About when I was living in my mother's house. You wanted to know if I had ever been a—"

"What are you talking about? I was not about to ask that."

"Then what were you trying to ask me?"

"If . . . when you lived in your mother's house if any of the men ever tried to, well, interfere with you. It was start-ing to sink in how mean your childhood was, how vulner-able you were."

Victoria was stunned.

Wyatt took her hands in his. "I am truly, truly sorry, Victoria. I was beastly. I was caught off guard when I am so used to being on top of things. I . . . was wrong. I can imagine what a burden it is to live with such a secret. What

I want more than anything else is to shoulder some of that burden."

From his waistcoat pocket Wyatt brought out the emerald-and-diamond ring. "I have been carrying it around with me since that day, hoping to run into you, working up the courage to pay you a visit, then when I heard you had gone to Baltimore, I—"

Victoria stared at him unblinking. "You what, Wyatt?"

"I hoped that when you came back . . ."

WISHES HAVING WINGS

"Dearly beloved, we are gathered here today . . ."

As Reverend James A. Handy spoke, eighteen-year-old Victoria chose to go back.

Not to Factors Row.

Not to that house on Minis Street.

Not to the uncles.

She went back to Wyatt's tearful pleadings for forgiveness.

Back to how crushed he looked when she said she needed time to think.

Back to cut flowers he sent.

Back to making him wait.

Back to wanting to be sure.

Back to their splendid dinner at Wormley's.

". . . in holy matrimony, which is an honorable estate . . ."

Back to dizzying days of choosing cakes and canapés.

"... or forever hold their peace."

Back to the evening Dorcas Vashon informed her that she would soon be on her way, taking Mr. and Mrs. Rodgers with her, and then gave her five hundred dollars for her Mothers' Helpers club.

Back to tears and the coded way that they would keep in touch.

Back to Dorcas Vashon telling her that it was now fine to write Ma Clara.

"I am confident that the two of you will be discreet, wise," she said, then revealed that through Miss Abby, Clara Wiggins knew the mission that she was on.

"She asked me to give you a helping hand."

"You mean—"

"Yes, before you asked me to meet with her."

"But when?"

"One day when you and Binah went marketing."

Back to processing just how much she owed Ma Clara.

Back to dashing off that first letter.

Back to beholding Madame Keckley's sketch of her champagne wedding dress: "Open high wing-tip collar ... close-fitting bodice ... twelve satin buttons ... one side of the dress will sweep up into a bunting drape ... an under-skirt of bead-flecked lace ... entire outfit adorned with intricately beaded champagne appliqués ... copious layers of ruffled satin and beaded lace form the edge of a four-foot train."

Back to, moments ago, the butterflies in her stomach as the pitch-perfect organ pealed forth into Mendelssohn's magisterial march composed for a scene in *A Midsummer Night's Dream.*

"I now pronounce you . . ."

Back to wishes having wings.

Victoria went forward too. To a future with a family of her own, praying doubly hard for at least one daughter.

If so blessed, she vowed to name her of all things . . .

Savannah.

AUTHOR'S NOTE

Months after my novel *Crossing Ebenezer Creek* was published I began to wonder about my characters, other than
Caleb, who survived the journey.

What happened to them?

What, who did they become?

Their offspring?

Inventing Victoria arose from this curiosity. I seized upon
a minor character in *Crossing Ebenezer Creek*, Praline, and
began *my* journey, a journey into the life of a girl born during Reconstruction, a time when positive forces were at
work to make America live up to its ideals—when slavery
was abolished, when black people became US citizens, when
black men gained the right to the national vote. But then . . .

Gains, strides toward true democracy were crushed.
White supremacy triumphed.

Still, against the odds many black people persevered,

more than a few thrived. And *Inventing Victoria* became a journey into a rather neglected aspect of black history: the black middle class and black aristocracy of the past. Besides Frederick Douglass, the black strivers, black successes who appear in Victoria's world in person and by mention include West Point cadet Johnson C. Whittaker, Booker T. Washington, John Wesley Cromwell, John Deveaux, Daniel Alexander Payne Murray, John Mercer Langston, James Wormley, Elizabeth Keckley, Henry E. Baker, Madam Selika, the Fisk Jubilee Singers, Mary "Mollie" Church Terrell, George Boyer Vashon, Samuel and Alice Proctor, Peter and George Downing, and Reverend Handy, Metropolitan AME Church. And oh, yes, Orindatus Simon Bolívar Wall!

Also out of history are the astrologer Madam Smith, James Jefferson's Barber Saloon, JP Kendy's grocery store, Eugene Morehead's Forest City Bar and Restaurant, and Clapp's 99 Cents Store.

Out of history came other small things as well. For example, according to the 1880 US Federal Census Savannah had at least one Scriven and one Bogins. There was a Jane Scriven "keeping house" and the laundress Josephine Bogins. That's how I came up with the gravediggers' names. On that same census page I found an Emma King and Katy Taylor, living on Minis Street. For both, in the column for occupation there was "prostitute."

I looked to history for other characters too. Abby

Bowfield is based on Rachel Brownfield (1833–1884), a woman who while still in slavery leased a mansion on Bryan Street and turned it into a boardinghouse that was eventually quite fine. "The 18-by-30-foot dining room was covered with an ingrain woolen carpet and featured a large leafed mahogany dining table," says David T. Dixon in his article "The Wealthiest Slave in Savannah: Rachel Brownfield and the True Price of Freedom."

Dorcas Vashon was inspired, in part, by Georgia's first black nun, Mother Mathilda Beasley (1832–1903), who went about doing so much good. Among other things, she founded Savannah's St. Francis Home for Colored Orphans, an institution for girls.

Dorcas Vashon's ancestry is based on that of Robert, Willam, and Joseph Purvis. The wealthy Robert Purvis, who spent most of his life in Philadelphia, Pennsylvania, cofounded the American Anti-Slavery Society (1833). He married Harriet Forten, a daughter of another wealthy Philadelphian, sailmaker James Forten. One of Robert and Harriet's children is the Dr. Charles Purvis mentioned in *Inventing Victoria.*

At times I took liberties with history. The March 21, 1882, issue of the DC's *Evening Star* announced that Frederick Douglass would give a lecture on John Brown at Bethel Hall that night. As I found no transcript of this lecture I used the speech Douglass gave on John Brown at West Virginia's Storer College in late May 1881. Also,

Henry E. Baker did give a lecture on "Originality" for the Monday Night Literary Club in the spring of 1882, but it was not held at Frederick Douglass's Cedar Hill (though Cedar Hill did host this club's events at times). For Baker's lecture I borrowed from his book *The Colored Inventor: A Record of Fifty Years*, published in 1913.

Some other tidbits: Merchants and Miners is the company that called itself "Queen of Sea Routes," and it purchased the *Saragossa* in the 1870s. The books Victoria beheld in Frederick Douglass's library come from the National Park Service's list of what it believes to be the vast majority of books that Douglass owned. You can check out this list at https://www.nps.gov/frdo/learn/historyculture /upload/Books-in-FDs-library.pdf.

The other items Victoria gazes upon come from my taking a virtual tour of the library at the Frederick Douglass National Historic Site.

The lawsuits challenging segregation that Victoria and Wyatt discuss were real and Wyatt was prescient. Shortly after they marry, on October 15, 1883, the US Supreme Court will declare the Civil Rights Act of 1875 unconstitutional. In 1896 comes the *Plessy* decision in which the high court will sanction segregation in places of public accommodation such as hotels, restaurants, theaters, and schools. In 1913 President Woodrow Wilson will give the green light to segregation in federal agencies. From office space and restrooms to cafeterias, black civil servants will be humiliated by Jim Crow.

Victoria and Wyatt's children will grow up in a very different DC.

Along with nineteenth-century newspapers, magazines, and ladies' books I am indebted to *Black Savannah, 1788–1864* by Whittington B. Johnson (Fayetteville: University of Arkansas Press, 1996) and *Saving Savannah: The City and the Civil War* by Jacqueline Jones (New York: Vintage, 2009), both of which I first read while at work on *Crossing Ebenezer Creek.* I am also indebted to Lawrence Otis Graham's *The Senator and the Socialite: The True Story of America's First Black Dynasty* (New York: Harper Perennial, 2007), Jacqueline M. Moore's *Leading the Race: The Transformation of the Black Elite in the Nation's Capital, 1880–1920* (Charlottesville: University of Virginia Press, 1999), and Elizabeth Dowling Taylor's *The Original Black Elite: Daniel Murray and the Story of a Forgotten Era* (New York: Amistad, 2017).

History!

What a journey!

RESEARCH AND SOURCES

Page 18 "Freewillum": Lydia Parrish. *Slave Songs of the Georgia Sea Islands* (Athens: University of Georgia Press, 1992), p. 46.

Page 42 "At six o'clock yesterday . . . cut off": *Savannah Morning News*, April 7, 1880, p. 2.

Page 85 The woman who left $750 for the religious instruction of black people in Georgia was Henrietta Parker of New Britain, Connecticut: *Colored Tribune*, April 1, 1876, p. 2.

Page 86 On the murder of an old man named John: "Another Willful Murder—Where Is It to End?" *Colored Tribune*, March 11, 1876, p. 3. The black man's last name was Daniel. His killers were James and John Graham.

Page 90 "Deed to the house on Minis Street": based on a deed of conveyance from M. J. McKnitt to

M. B. L. Ramsey, October 2, 1882, http://dlc.lib.utk
.edu/spc/view?docId=tei/0012_000060_000502_0000
/0012_000060_000502_0000.xml.

Page 131 "Air Brick. . . . Charlton House, Kent": Isabella
Beeton. *Beeton's Housewife's Treasury of Domestic
Information* (London: Ward, Lock & Co, between 1879
and 1890), p. xxv.

Page 131 "Position gives power. . . . and healthful
position": Platt R. Spencer. *Spencerian Key to Practical
Penmanship* (New York: Ivison, Phinney, Blakeman &
Co., 1866), p. 24.

Page 138 pä-ˌtā-də-ˌfwä-ˈgrä: pronunciation guide is
from *Merriam Webster's*, online edition, https://www
.merriam-webster.com/dictionary/pâté%20de%20
foie%20gras.

Page 149 *A-bate' . . . As-sid'u-ous-ly*: pronunciation guide
from Noah Webster's *An American Dictionary of the
English Language*. Revised by Chauncey A. Goodrich
and Noah Porter (Springfield, MA: G. & C. Merriam,
1865), pp. 2, 9, 20, 33, 84.

Page 150 "Visiting dress of purple plush. . . . elephant silk
and camel's hair." *Godey's Lady's Book and Magazine*,
December 1880, p. 586.

Page 150 "Do not pour coffee or tea. . . . excessively ill-
bred": Florence Hartley. *The Ladies' Book of Etiquette*
(Boston: Lee & Shepard, 1872), pp. 107, 110, 112, 114.

Page 162 Description of Wormley's Hotel: Carol
Gelderman. *A Free Man of Color and His Hotel: Race,*

Reconstruction, and the Role of the Federal Government (Washington, DC: Potomac Books Inc., 2012). Kindle.

Pages 176–177 "Not to fan the flame. . . . my good fortune to share": Frederick Douglass. *John Brown: An Address by Frederick Douglass at the Fourteenth Anniversary of Storer College of Harpers Ferry, West Virginia, May 30, 1881* (Dover, NH: Morning Star Job Printing House, 1881), p. 5.

Page 181 "There ought not to be anything. . . . originality of thought": Henry E. Baker. *The Colored Inventor: A Record of Fifty Years* (Project Gutenberg, 2007), e-book, p. 11.

Page 193 "Mr. Samuel Proctor has added. . . . perfect for archery and croquet": "Health and Pleasure," *People's Advocate*, May 21, 1881, p. 3.

Page 212 On the Victoria: "Fashion Notes," *People's Advocate*, November 26, 1881, p.1

Page 241 Invitation to the Fitzhugh Christmas gala: Based on a sample from Isabella Beeton. *Beeton's Housewife's Treasury of Domestic Information* (London: Ward, Lock & Co, between 1879 and 1890), p. 54.

ACKNOWLEDGMENTS

So grateful.

To *two* amazing, hardworking, probing, wonderful editors! First, Mary Kate Castellani, and then, when she went on leave, Susan Dobinick. The transition was absolutely painless, so seamless.

I also had the good, great fortune to work with the assiduous, thoughtful, and so very engaged copyeditor Patricia McHugh, proofreader Regina Castillo, and production editor Diane Aronson. I am also grateful to so many others at Bloomsbury for their hard work and support: Claire Stetzer, Beth Eller, Courtney Griffin, Brittany Mitchell, Donna Mark, Melissa Kavonic, Cindy Loh, and Cristina Gilbert.

Huge thanks is due my sister, Nelta, a graduate of FIT, who was super helpful with descriptions of clothing, especially the really fancy items. I also thank L. J. Dean with the National Railway Historical Society for the generous response to my questions about the Baltimore & Potomac Railroad and to Brittany Mayo at the Georgia Historical Society for the swift response to my inquiry about Shad Island.

Thanks, too, to Sharon G. Flake for sound, solid feedback on the early manuscript.

And to my agent, Jennifer Lyons: as always you have been matchless.